Martha's Long Winter

Written by Bekah O'Brien
Illustrated by Bethany O'Brien

Dedication:

To Jesus, my Friend and Savior, without whom I could not write these stories; as well as all of my friends who have prayed for and supported me throughout the process of writing these books.

Matthew 10:29-31

"Are not two sparrows sold for a farthing? and one of them shall not fall on the ground without your Father. But the very hairs of your head are all numbered. Fear ye not therefore, ye are of more value than many sparrows."

Psalm 28:7

The LORD is my strength and my shield; my heart trusted in him, and I am helped: therefore my heart greatly rejoiceth; and with my song will I praise him."

Chapters

The Knight Family:
Peter Knight (Dad)
Rosemary Knight (Mom)
Children:
Martha Knight (age 13)
Thomas Knight (age 11)
Twins: James Knight (age 9)
Anna Knight (age 9)
Lydia Knight (age 5)
Sarah Knight (age 3)
Elizabeth Knight (age 1)

Chapter 1
At the Ball

It was a cold winter day in 1930 and thirteen-year-old Martha Knight was gathering wood from the stack alongside the house. She shivered as she bent down and grabbed a log and put it in the crook of her arm.

She repeated this several times and when she had enough, she headed toward the back door which led to the kitchen. She knocked on the door with her foot since her arms were full and couldn't open it.

Rosemary Knight, Martha's mom, came and opened the door and pulled her daughter in.

"Burrr.... it's freezing cold outside. I can't feel my fingers anymore," exclaimed Martha. She dumped the cold wood into the wood box and went to stand near the fire in the living room while her mother finished the afternoon meal. She stuck her hands out to the warmth and sighed as her fingers began to tingle.

A few minutes later, when she felt cozy and warm inside, she unbuttoned her coat and went to the kitchen to help her mother set the table for lunch.

Martha's sisters Anna, Lydia, and Sarah were already in the warm room and were setting the table. One-year-old Elizabeth was trying to climb up in her high chair, but was unsuccessful and fell to the ground.

Martha walked over and picked up her sister and helped her into her chair. Elizabeth Knight was almost two now and was learning to walk, but was still clumsy on her feet. Martha patted her rosy cheeks and went to help her Mom get the chili on the table.

"Can I help you with anything, Mom?" Martha asked.

"Yes, you can. Would you please take these full bowls of chili to the table for me? I don't want your sisters carrying them."

"Okay," Martha assented happily as she lifted the bowls two by two and carried them to the table where the silverware and napkins were set neatly in their places. She heard a tell-tale sign of giggling that sounded as if it came from under the table. She bent down and saw three of her sisters under it. "What are you doing under here?" she questioned.

"We were going to try to scare you." said five-year-old Lydia, trying hard to put on her most scary face.

"I'm glad you didn't, because you might have upset the bowls of chili I had just set on the table."

"Oh, then, we are too." assured Sarah, licking her lips.

"You had better take your seats so that you don't cause anymore mischief."

"All right, Martha," replied her sisters.

Just as Martha got up from bending down under the table, another gust of wind swooped into the kitchen from the back door and what it blew in was quite a sight.

Peter Knight, with both of his sons standing on either side of him, looked like snowmen; they had come in from the barn. "It started snowing pretty hard, so the boys and I decided to rig a rope to the barn and the house so we can do the evening chores."

"That's good, sweetheart." Mom answered. "Lunch is just about ready, so if you want to go to the living room, hang up your coats and warm yourselves up, I'll have it all ready."

"Okay, dear, sounds great," Dad replied and quickly kissed her cheek.

Eleven-year-old Thomas and nine-year-old James followed him, leaving behind them a trail of slushy snow that had started to melt from their boots. Martha quickly swept it up and sat at the table, where the boys soon joined them.

"Let's pray," said Dad, bowing his head.

"Dear Father in Heaven, thank You for this delicious meal that the ladies have made for us. Please help us all be thankful for what You have given to us. Please help us to share what we have with others. In Your Name, amen."

They all started eating and enjoying the meal that their Lord had blessed them with and ate slowly.

"Dad, will we still be able to go to the Christmas ball tonight?" questioned Martha a bit anxiously.

"I think so. A little snow isn't going to stop the Knight family is it?"

Martha giggled at the 'little' snow. Truth be told, the snow had been knee deep for the last two weeks and it wasn't getting better.

"What time are Mr. and Mrs. Williams coming for you?" asked Mom.

"I think about six. That'll give us a good hour to get there. It's about five miles east of where we live."

There was a Christmas ball that night and Thomas and Martha were going with the Williams family in their sleigh. This ball was every year on

the first Saturday in December. They did dances
from the Civil War period. Martha was excited
about it, but Thomas, you could say, was not as
enthusiastic about it as his sister; he didn't care if
he went or not. So that made the decision easier for
his parents.

After lunch, Martha and her sisters, Anna
and Lydia, did the dishes. Martha washed them,
Lydia dried them, and Anna put them away in the
cabinets. "I wish I could go," said Anna with a little
pout.

"Remember what Mom and Dad said? You
can go next year with us."

"I know, but I can't help but think I'll be
missing out on some fun."

Martha felt bad for her sister, so she said, "I'll
tell you what; tomorrow, maybe, I can arrange for a
practice ball during the fellowship time at church.
How does that sound?"

"Would you really?" asked Anna.

"You bet I would," replied Martha.

"Thanks sis," rejoiced Anna, hugging her
around her waist.

The sisters went into the living room where
the others were. Martha brought along her school

books so she could study for a test by the fire, sitting far enough away so the few sparks that flew here and there wouldn't catch on her books.

She was taking notes from her history book when a small, chubby, hand lay upon it and tore the page. "Elizabeth! No!"

Elizabeth sat back in surprise with the paper clutched in her hand. Martha calmed herself and asked, "Elizabeth, would you give that back to me, please?"

Elizabeth reluctantly gave back the paper. Martha sighed, and as she straightened out the paper said, "Elizabeth, would you please forgive me for yelling at you?"

"Yes," replied Elizabeth.

She finished her notes, closed her history book and got out her math. She was behind in that subject and was trying to catch back up. That's why she was doing school during the weekend.

After she was finished with her school it was three o'clock and she needed to start getting ready. Mom got the wash tub and filled it with the water she had been warming on the stove and Martha took her bath, then Thomas took his.

Martha went upstairs to her room and when she opened the closed door, Jubilee, Martha's kitten, rushed out and went downstairs. Martha shook her head and wondered what fix her little cat would get herself into next.

She curled her hair with a heated iron till at long last there was an array of brown curls dangling down to her waist. She pinned it back so it wouldn't get in the way, and then put her dress on. She was wearing the same dress that she wore to her parents' party that they had had in August.

She buttoned up the back and twirled herself before the mirror. The candle light flooded gently across her face and hair and made her look quite elegant.

She stood there for a moment until she finally heard the gentle ringing of bells on a sleigh. She hurriedly put on her gloves and got her coat and scarf and hurried down the stairs just as Dad opened the door.

"Good evening, Williams family, wonderful night, isn't it?"

"Yes, it is, Peter. Are your children ready to leave?" asked Mr. Aaron Williams.

"Indeed they are," responded Dad, as Thomas shrugged into his coat and offered his sister his arm and went to the sleigh to join the rest of the small group.

"Martha, you look exquisite!" exclaimed Rose Williams.

"Thank you. You two belles look wonderful!"

They climbed into the sleigh and after Mr. Williams hopped in beside his wife and daughter, Rose, he clucked to the horses and the sleigh leaped forward and they were off.

Martha clenched her teeth as the falling snow flew into their faces, but she got used to it. Five minutes into the ride, they started singing: "Jingle bells, jingle bells, jingle all the way!" Oh, this was going to be great fun!

About an hour later, the sleigh stopped in front of the ballroom door and Mr. Williams helped them out and said, "I'm going to go put the horses in the stable. I'll be there in a moment." Thomas opened the wooden door for the ladies and they all stepped into the warm front room.

The building was in three separate rooms. There was the front room which had a fire place withd a few chairs in front of it. Cathryn spotted a few tree racks to hang their coats and scarves on. Then there was the ballroom itself and another small room which held all the pastries and punch.

Thomas and the others took off their coats and went and stood as near to the fireplace as they dared. Martha rubbed her arms. "Boy, that was a cold ride, although it was very fun. I'm glad to be warming up now."

Once they were all toasty warm inside, Cathryn suggested they go and get some hot chocolate.

"Sounds good to me," replied Martha, as she linked her arm with Cathryn's.

"Four hot chocolates, please," spoke Rose as the lady in charge of the buffet poured two cups of punch for another couple.

The foursome drank their warm hot cocoa and the girls pointed out what dresses looked pretty. Then, it was time to start dancing.

As the caller called for them to find their partners for the Virginia Reel, Harry Kate came up and said, "May I have the pleasure of the Virginia Reel, Miss Knight?"

"Yes, you may," replied Martha as she handed him her dance card and he handed her his. Martha put her name on it, then he offered her his arm; she took it and they went out to the dance floor.

Thomas danced with Rose, and Cathryn danced with a young man Martha didn't recognize, but they were all in the same group.

"Ladies and gentlemen!" started the caller, "the Virginia Reel."

All the couples bowed and curtsied to each other and the dance began.

After the first set, they all regrouped and hurried to get a drink and to fill their dance cards for the next set of four dances.

Before they knew it, the caller was calling the next dance which was the 'Polka', a very lively dance, which was also one of Martha's favorites. She danced this one with Bruce Gates and they had great fun. A few girls lost their shoes due to the fast pace, but thankfully, Martha held onto hers. At the end of that set Cathryn came up and said, "I've lost my shoe!"

"Well, let me help you find it then," Martha offered.

So they split up and searched high and low, but couldn't find it. Then they heard a loud voice speaking over the crowd. "Attention! A lady has lost her shoe. Please come to the front room to retrieve it."

Cathryn broke out into an embarrassed laugh and, with rosy cheeks, went to get her shoe.

The next set began and Martha danced the 'Gallop' with a boy named Titus whom she didn't know, but seemed very nice. And so began the third set. Martha was having great fun. She didn't want it to end. She just wanted to keep on dancing and dancing and dancing until her aching feet just fell off. She would never forget her first ball.

Before Martha knew it, the ball was over and she stood with Cathryn and Rose and some other girls in a group while Thomas said his goodbyes.

Finally, it was time to head home and the girls put on their coats and scarves and waited by the door for Mr. Williams. When the sleigh came, the girls said goodbye and they climbed into the sleigh and pulled the blankets up around them. It had been fun and now they were heading home. Martha couldn't wait to tell her sisters all about it.

When the sleigh arrived at her door, Martha thanked Mr. and Mrs. Williams for letting her and Thomas ride with them and said goodbye to Cathryn and Rose. Martha could still hear the bells on the horses' harness jingling as the Williams' went home.

Martha took off her coat and warmed by the fire. Her parents were nowhere in sight. But then she heard soft talking that came from the kitchen, so she went and said goodnight to her parents. After promising that she would tell all about it at breakfast the next morning, she hurried and got ready for bed.

Even though she could barely keep her eyes open, she wanted to record this evening in her diary while it was still fresh in her mind. So she got her pencil and her diary and sat down at the desk in her room and started writing.

December 4th, 1930

Dear God,

I had so much fun tonight. The Christmas ball was tonight and the Williams' were more than happy to take Thomas and me with them. Oh, it was such great fun. Everyone looked their best and looked like they were having the time of their life. It was SO much fun and I can't wait to go next year, hopefully. Thank You for blessing me with this opportunity to have an experience I will never forget. I think my favorite dance tonight was the 'Polka'.

Well, I can barely keep my eyes open, so I think I'll go to bed now. I love You, Jesus.

Your daughter,

Martha Rosemary Knight

The next morning was a hustle for Martha. She woke up later than usual since she got home so late. But she hurried downstairs just as everyone sat down to breakfast.

"Good morning, Martha," greeted Mom. "Did you sleep well?"

"Like a baby," replied Martha, with a last yawn and sat down at her chair between Anna and Lydia.

"Let's pray," said Dad, bowing his head.

"Dear Father, thank You for getting Martha and Thomas home safely. Please protect us today as we go to church; thank You for this meal and please bless the hands that prepared it. In Your Name we pray; amen."

Everyone started to pass around the plate of pancakes that were stacked high. As the plate came toward her, Anna asked, "Did you have a fun time? What was it like?"

"Yes, I had a wonderful time. To describe it to you, let's see here. The room was illuminated by candles and there was a big chandelier hanging above. It was very beautiful."

"It sounds like you had great fun."

"Yes, I did."

"Girls, why don't you eat your breakfast? I know you're excited, but we need to leave for church in an hour and the table needs to be cleared," said Dad.

"Yes, sir," and they focused on their meal.

"Martha, are you almost ready?" asked Mom.

"Yes, ma'am," replied Martha, as she finished tying Elizabeth's bonnet. She picked her up and hurried outside where the wagon and the rest of the family were waiting for her. Making sure she closed the door, she went and lifted Elizabeth into her mother's lap and sat down in the back of the wagon with her siblings.

"Are we still going to dance, Martha?" asked Anna anxiously.

"Sure we are. I promised you we would, didn't I?"

"Yes."

"Then a promise is a promise. We'll probably do it after we finish eating lunch."

"Okay, thanks, Martha."

"You're welcome," Martha smiled at her sister, glad she could do something to please her.

About a half hour later, they arrived at church. They went in and seated themselves and Martha asked her parents if she could go visit with her friends.

After gaining permission from her parents, she hurried across the room where her friends were talking.

"Hi Martha," greeted Polly McShire.

"Hello, how are you today?"

"We're doing okay. Are you coming to the fundraiser next Sunday?"

"No, I don't think so. I would love to, but it's Elizabeth's birthday and I believe we're coming to church, but I don't think we're staying for lunch."

"Maybe you could stay with us," said Polly.

"Maybe; I'll ask my Mom after church."

"All right, then, make sure you do."

Martha smiled at her friend as she started to her seat because the service was about to start.

"Good morning. I hope you all are doing well. Please stand and turn to number three in your hymnal."

After church was done and Martha's siblings went to play with their friends, Martha went to find her parents, who were talking to the pastor, Michael Share. She placed her arm on her Mom's shoulder and waited politely for her parents to notice her.

"Where's Janelle today? Is she feeling well?" asked Mom with concern.

"No, she didn't sleep too well last night. She's gotten over the morning sickness, I think, but the baby was moving around last night, so I told her to stay home and rest."

"Well, tell her that if she needs any help, or needs a meal, just let us know."

"Okay, thanks."

"You're welcome. Who's going to deliver the baby?"

"Leslie McShire, I believe, is going to deliver him."

"Him? Are you sure it's a boy? It could be a girl," said Dad teasingly.

"You're right. My wife has warned me, too. We really don't care if it's a boy or a girl, just as long as he or she is healthy. I don't know why I keep calling the baby 'him', though."

"Well, Leslie McShire is a great midwife. She delivered my three youngest daughters."

"I have great confidence in Leslie's abilities.

Now, if you'll excuse me, I need to be getting home to see if my wife needs anything." The pastor excused himself and Martha's parents turned toward her.

"What is it, dear?" asked Mom.

"Well, you know there is going to be a fundraiser next Sunday to build a bigger orphanage in Boulder, Montana. Since we won't be going because of Elizabeth's birthday, may I go with Polly? She asked me to."

"Well," said Mom undecidedly. She looked toward Dad and raised an eyebrow in question.

"Martha," started Dad.

"Please?" interrupted Martha.

"Martha, it's rude to interrupt," Mom corrected.

Martha winced, "Sorry Dad."

"I forgive you. Now about the fundraiser, I'm going to say no. It's your sister's birthday and I think this would be a good lesson in putting family first."

Martha bit her tongue to keep from coaxing and said, "Yes, Dad."

Polly could tell by the look on her friend's face what her parents' decision must have been. "Your parents said no?"

"Yes, Daddy said we need to put Elizabeth first since it's her birthday, and I suppose he's right, although I really wanted to go."

"Well, I'm sure you'll still have fun celebrating your sister's birthday."

"Yes, I'm sure I will." replied Martha, trying to cheer up.

"She's turning two, right?"

"Yes."

"Can you believe it, Martha? Already TWO years have passed since your sister was born?"

"Yes. She's growing up quickly."

"Come on. Let's go get some lunch before the boys get all of it," Polly joked.

As Martha headed toward the food table, her heart still wasn't right, *Dear Lord, my heart isn't right. Please replace this feeling with joy for another year with my baby sister.*

Amazingly, her heart did seem lighter and more cheerful. She hurried to catch up with her friend.

After lunch, she organized a group that wanted to dance and Martha, despite her slightly sore feet, had fun.

Chapter 2
Family First

The next Sunday, it was snowing furiously and Martha woke to the sound of wind roaring outside her window. She decided that it would be best if she went ahead and got up, so she took a deep breath and quickly got out of the bed and hurriedly tip toed to her dresser, got her clothes, and went down to the kitchen to dress by the fire. "Are the boys here?"

"You're up early. It's only five-thirty, but you're safe, the boys are out in the barn."

"I woke up to the wind and decided to get up."

"Oh, I see," replied Mom, not taking her eyes off the pot of oatmeal she was stirring.

Martha got dressed, then put her coat and scarf on and prepared to go out to the barn.

"Be careful out there. It's easy for a body to get lost."

"I will." Giving her mother a kiss, she opened the door and turned her face away from the snow that pelted against her skin.

She shivered and hurried toward the barn, grabbing the rope at the end of the porch railing.

Once she got to the end of the long rope, she opened the door with a little effort and stepped inside.

The hay smelled sweet and rich this time of year and offered much warmth. Dad sat on a stool and was milking Cassie, their cow, James was raking hay from the loft, and Thomas was feeding their horses, Zoe and Vernon. Martha walked over to Thomas and petted Zoe on the nose. "Good morning."

"Good morning, Martha. Does Zoe look a little strange to you?" questioned Thomas.

"Hmm," thought Martha, taking a half step backward and looking at the mare. "She does look like she's been eating a little too much lately. Better cut down on the oats, girl," she admonished, coming to a conclusion and patting her on the forehead.

"You may want to feel her belly, Martha," said Dad, turning toward her and winking at Thomas.

Confused, Martha placed her hand on the mare's stomach and waited. "I don't feel anything. It's maybe a little bigger."

"Keep your hand there and see if you feel anything," Dad persisted.

Suddenly, she felt something move in Zoe's

middle, and then Martha caught on. "You mean...you mean...Zoe's pregnant?!"

"Yes, that's exactly what I mean, and I'm glad you finally caught on," Dad chuckled warmly.

Martha hugged the mare around her neck and Zoe tossed her head and whinnied.

"Vernon and Zoe will probably be parents by late April." Dad added jovially.

"You mean she's been carrying this baby for a few months already?"

"Yes, I believe so," said Dad matter-of-factly.

"Why didn't you tell me?"

"Because I wasn't sure, and I didn't want to waste money on a doctor, but now I know for sure. I didn't want you to get your hopes up just in case it wasn't true."

"I can't believe it! You're going to be a papa sometime soon ol' pal." Martha patted Vernon on the rump.

"Martha, you'd better get to the chickens. It's already six o'clock and breakfast will be on in an hour."

"Yes, Dad," and she went off and filled her

bowl with chicken feed and threw the food down on the barn floor where the chickens stayed during winter.

They pecked the ground with their little beaks and then made way for their leader, an older rooster who could be quite bossy. The Knight family affectionately called him Ol' Red.

Martha dumped the rest of the food on the ground and headed out the door. "See you guys at breakfast." She hurried out to the house.

She burst into the back door, bringing an arm load of wood for the fire and exclaimed, "Zoe's going to have a filly!"

"Are you sure it won't be a foal?" said her mother with a soft smile playing at the corners of her mouth. Martha didn't pay attention to it. "I think it'll be a filly."

"We'll see. I'm nearly as excited about it as you are. The foal will be here just in time for spring." Mom replied, trying not to laugh. "Go wake your sisters."

Martha put up her coat and headed upstairs. She gently shook her siblings and said, "Guess what?"

"What?" asked Anna, "is it time to get up already?"

"Yes, but that's not all. Zoe's gonna have a baby."

"She is?"

"Yes, isn't that exciting?"

"Yay! Zoe's gonna have a baby!" squealed Lydia.

By now all three of her sisters were dancing around the room and Elizabeth pulled herself up in her crib and started laughing at her sisters' enthusiasm.

"Martha!" called Mom, "I asked you to wake your sisters, not to bring the house down!"

"Sorry Mom; come on girls. Get dressed in your best for church today."

"Okay," said her sisters in unison with smiles all over their faces.

Martha went over and picked her baby sister up and set her on the bed to dress her. Then it dawned on her that today was her sister's birthday. Elizabeth was turning two today. "Happy Birthday, Elizabeth!" she exclaimed.

Her sister just clapped her hands, stomped her feet and yelled at the top of her lungs 'mama' because that was the only word she knew. Her family was working on her vocabulary, but so far, they weren't getting anywhere with her.

Martha took Elizabeth's hand and let her walk slowly and helped her up when she stumbled.

They made it down the hall and her big sister carried her down the stairs and into her high chair, where she cooed her good morning to her mom. Mom pinched her cheek, kissed her, and gave her a cracker.

Ten minutes later, the family sat down to breakfast and Dad said the prayer. After the blessing, Dad announced, "Today is a very special day. Two years ago, God gave us a wonderful blessing. He gave us a wonderful daughter and sister named Elizabeth Kathleen Knight. We are very thankful He put her in this family. Today we are going to have a celebration. We will have cake and a few presents, and we'll also have a few games that everyone, including the birthday girl, can play. How does that sound?"

"Great!"

"We'll have a special lunch after church. It'll be a little late, but I think we'll be fine." A minute later, he added, "We'll need to leave in about an hour, so we need to eat our breakfast so we can get ready."

"Yes, Dad."

After they got back home from church, Martha went to her room to put her Bible away. Then she put her apron on and helped her Mom with lunch.

There was going to be fried chicken, fresh bread, and birthday cake. "You can get started on frying the chicken." Mom offered to her daughter.

"All right." Martha got to work skinning the chicken and preparing it for the skillet. She had just placed the last leg of chicken into the frying pan and had wiped the grease off her hands, onto her apron as her Mom asked, "Do you still wish you could go to that fundraiser?"

"Part of me still does, but I'm kinda glad that I'm staying home. It's better to put family first, and then events."

Mom smiled to herself, glad that her daughter felt that way.

"Can you believe that Elizabeth is turning two, already? It seems that just yesterday she was born and I held her in my arms for the first time," Martha expressed dreamily.

"I know. It's hard to believe. I'm glad God saw fit to put her into our lives. She's a blessing to us all. I hope He gives us another."

"Me too," replied Martha.

"But, I'm also looking forward to having a few grandchildren in a few years," said Mom, poking Martha in the ribs.

"A few years! I'm only thirteen. I think it'll be a LONG time before I get married."

"Don't underestimate that. It will be here before you know it."

"Don't worry. I won't. Maybe when I'm thirty, I'll think about it more," replied Martha, playfully.

"We'll see," was the simple reply from her mother.

An hour later, everyone was sitting around the table, ready for Elizabeth's birthday celebration. Dad placed Elizabeth in her high chair and put the bib around her neck, for he had a feeling this was going to be VERY messy.

Mom brought the cake in, set it in the middle of the table and placed two candles in the center of the cake and lit them.

Everyone began the song. "Happy Birthday to you! Happy Birthday to you! Happy Birthday, dear Elizabeth, Happy Birthday to you!"

Mom cut the cake and gave the first slice to Elizabeth. The two-year-old stared at it a minute, but as all toddlers do, dug her hands right into the cake! She stuck her finger in her mouth and her eyes widened in surprise at the taste of it.

She scooped another handful into her mouth and chewed it. Everyone laughed at her messy face with chocolate icing all over. Once she finished her plate, she held it out with her two chubby hands and said, "More."

"Wow!" the boys exclaimed, "she said her first word!"

"It could have been more polite, but with time, she'll learn," laughed Mom as she placed another small sliver of cake onto her daughter's plate.

After cake, there were presents. Elizabeth ripped open the small package and she looked in awe at her gift. It was a beaded necklace that the younger girls had made for her. Mom put it around her neck and the young girl could not take her eyes off it.

Martha handed her a present and she took it in her small hands. She opened it and saw a small stuffed doll that Martha had made herself. She clutched the doll to her chest and babbled in her baby talk that was all too familiar with her.

"Let's play a few games," said Dad, as Mom started to clear the table, the wrapping paper littered all over.

Everyone adjourned to the living room where they played "fishing." Elizabeth held a small fishing rod with a hook, and with the help of Martha, maneuvered the hook into a box. James, who was chosen to help out for this game, put a little prize at the end of the hook and up came a little box and inside the box was a small wooden animal that looked like a horse that Dad had made.

"Hoss!" She squealed in excitement.

Her family was amazed. Here they were trying to teach her words for the past year, and NOW she chose to use them, especially on her birthday!

After that game, Martha helped out with the next one while Thomas helped Elizabeth. While Martha was helping, she thought, *I'm glad I stayed home.*

Later that evening, when Dad went out to do the evening barn chores, Martha asked if she could go along. Lydia and Sarah had asked Mom to let them go and see Zoe.

So Martha helped them with their coats and scarves and they all went out to the barn. Dad set to milking Cassie and Martha had agreed to feed the horses so Thomas and James could finish up some school work they needed to finish before the new school week started.

While Martha got the oats for Vernon and Zoe, Lydia crawled up on the side of the stall and, with chin in hand, stared at the growing tummy while Sarah squeezed in and petted Zoe. "Be careful, Sarah." Martha warned gently. "I don't want her to accidentally kick you."

"Okay, Martha," replied Sarah, stepping out of the stall and joining Lydia on the stall railing.

Martha dumped the feed into Zoe's trough and the mare bent her head down and the girls could hear her chewing the oats that tasted so good to the mare.

Martha got the same for Vernon and as Martha finished feeding him, set to brushing them to make their coats soft and shiny. Martha noticed Sarah seemed deep in thought. "What are you thinking about, dearie?"

"I was thinking: how can a baby get in there?" asked Sarah, pointing to Zoe. "Who made her baby?"

"Well, God made the baby and put it in Zoe's tummy."

"It sure seems comp'cated. Wonder how He does that?"

Martha tried not to laugh, and replied, "Well, Sarah, I'm not sure how He does that either. I guess it's not for us to know. But I do know that God knows everything. And I know we can trust Him with things like that. Say goodnight to Zoe and we'll go to the house."

"Yes," replied Sarah.

The girls went to the house and after every one had gone to bed, Martha told her Mom about the conversation with her sister and they both had a good laugh over it.

Chapter 3
The Flu

Wednesday came, and the Knight family had just sat down at the table to eat lunch. Dad bowed his head to pray. "Dear Jesus, thank You for all You have given us. Please nourish this food to our bodies and please bless the hands that prepared it. Please help us to have a productive afternoon. In Your Name, amen."

Everyone dug into the meal and thanked Mom for it. They started into conversation and after everyone had finished eating Mom noticed that Sarah hadn't eaten much, if any, of her lunch. Her face was pale and she sat at the table with her chin in her hands, ignoring the rule they had about no elbows on the table. "Sarah, are you all right?" asked Mom.

"I don't feel well, Mommy. I have a headache and my stomach doesn't feel too well."

"Hmm," said Mom worriedly. "I hope it's not the flu."

"What's the flu, Mommy?"

"Oh, just a bug, honey."

"What kind of bug?"

"Never mind, it's just when you get sick—"

Mom thought for a minute and then said to her daughter, "I think you need to go to bed for some rest." She came over and put her hand on Sarah's forehead and exclaimed, "You have a fever. Come with me," leading her by the hand up the stairs. "Martha, please lead in lunch cleanup and then grab me some clean cloths and a bowl of cool water."

"Yes, ma'am," replied Martha gravely. She surely hoped this wasn't the flu. A doctor was hard to get in the winter with it being snowy.

Mom tucked Sarah into bed and went to a nearby chest in the corner, took out two extra quilts and tucked them around Sarah. She gladly took the quilts, shivered and asked, "Mommy, will I get better?"

"Of course you will; all you need is some rest."

And with that, Sarah closed her eyes and went to sleep.

About ten minutes later, Martha came up with the bowl of water and the rags.

"Thanks, Martha." Mom dipped the rags in water and took one, folded it up and placed it on the three year old's forehead.

After Mom finished, she turned toward Martha. "We're going to have to watch the others closely, Martha. I do believe it is the flu. I want you to take some blankets and pile them in the living room. I'm going to keep you healthy ones in there and the sick ones in here. It'll be easier to care for them. Come. I'll help you. My guess will be that Sarah doesn't wake again for a few hours."

"Okay Mom," replied Martha.

"Oh, and I want you and the others washing your hands often and thoroughly. Hopefully it will keep the sickness away. Don't worry about finishing your school. I want you to spend the rest of the day with your sisters and keep a close eye on them for the flu."

"Yes, ma'am," replied Martha, laying the blankets near the fire to help them stay warm for that night. Then she went and washed her hands.

Martha gathered her sisters and took them to the living room and played puzzles with them for a while. After they were bored with that, Martha read to them from her Bible.

After she finished the story of Ruth, Lydia, who was sitting in Martha's lap, announced that she didn't feel too well. Martha felt her forehead and sure enough, she had a fever, so she took her upstairs and tucked her into bed beside Sarah, put a cloth on her head and left her sleeping.

Martha was surprised to see her Mom not in with Sarah so she went looking for her. She decided to try in the boys' room. She knocked on the closed door and Mom stepped out. "James came in from the barn about ten minutes ago complaining of a headache. He's got the flu."

"That's not good. Lydia just came down with it herself. I put her in bed beside Sarah and put a cloth on her forehead." Just then, a voice from inside exclaimed, "Mom, I'm going to be sick!"

"Hurry, Martha, go and get a bowl, and while you're at it, get two for the girls' room just in case."

Martha hurried downstairs, got the bowls and returned and gave them to Mom. Then she headed back downstairs and stayed with her sisters.

Martha laid Elizabeth on the couch for a nap and tucked a blanket around her. Then she read quietly again to Anna. And finally, even Anna grew sleepy and rested her head on the arm of the chair and slept. Martha got out her knitting and worked on the scarf she was making for Thomas' Christmas present.

Martha was obedient and stayed with her sisters the whole rest of the day. She took them to the kitchen and Anna worked on her reading while Martha made a cold supper of sandwiches. She also took a few crackers and some water up to the boys' room, dropped them off and then went into the girls' room where Mom was and handed the tray to her. "I thought you might want to try to get a little food in them."

"Thank you, Martha. I'll try," replied Mom, taking the tray and placing it on the little table by the bed.

Martha went back downstairs. Dad and Thomas came in and sat down to their meal. "Sorry I couldn't make anything hot. Mom instructed me to watch the others."

"It's fine, Martha," said Dad finishing his prayer and taking his first bite into his sandwich.

By nine-thirty, two more got sick. They were down to Thomas, Mom, Elizabeth, and Martha. Dad had come down with it soon after doing the evening barn chores. Martha was eager to stay up with her brother and Mom and help tend to the sick ones, but Mom told her she and Thomas must lay down and sleep.

So Martha and Thomas lay down on the couch after making sure Elizabeth was nice and cozy on her floor bed.

Seeing that the curly-headed two-year-old slept peacefully and without any signs of the sickness, Martha curled up and went to sleep, but not before praying that her family would get well soon.

The next morning, Martha bundled up and went to help Thomas with the barn chores. While he fed the horses, Martha milked Cassie and fed the chickens. Then she headed to the house while Thomas finished in the barn.

Martha went into the kitchen and got breakfast started, which was real quick. As she was pouring the hot oatmeal into bowls, Mom came into the kitchen, rubbing her forehead. "Are you well, Mom?" asked Martha, concerned.

"Yes dear, I'm fine. My head is hurting a little bit, but I think it's from fatigue. After I finish eating some breakfast, I think I'll lie down and rest for a bit if you can handle the sick ones."

"Sure, Mom, sleep as long as you want."

"I'll probably lie down for about two hours and then I'll be as good as new. Oh, and before I forget to tell you, Elizabeth got sick last night. I put her in my room with your father."

"All right; it sure is spreading fast," Martha commented.

"Yes. I just hope no more of us get sick."

Mom sighed as she sat at the table and ate the bowl of oatmeal. Then she went to the couch to rest.

Thomas came into the kitchen from the barn and Martha and he ate quickly. Then they both got to work taking care of the sick patients.

Martha went into the girls' room hauling a bucket of cool water and new cloths. She took the old ones off of the young girls and put new ones on. Sarah woke up and lifted her feverish head. "Martha, will you get me some water?"

"Certainly." Martha got her sister a cool cup of water and lifted it to her lips and watched as she drank slowly. Then Sarah sighed as her head hit the pillow again and she fell asleep.

Martha got the old bucket and cloths and took them into the kitchen where she threw away the old water and put the cloths in some boiling water she had on the stove to help get rid of the germs.

She went up to her parents' room to check on Elizabeth and Dad.

Her Dad was awake when she stepped into the room. "Martha, Elizabeth is tossing in her little bed. Will you try to settle her down?"

"Yes, sir," said Martha, looking worriedly at her dad, for his eyes where swollen and red.

Martha went over to Elizabeth's little bed and knelt beside her and put her hands on her forehead. Martha was surprised at how hot it felt, compared to the others. She took a cloth and patted her cheeks and forehead. That seemed to sooth her and she fell asleep for the time being.

She gave Dad some water and then went back down to the kitchen. She heard her Mom groan as she got back up. She went to her and felt her forehead.

"You have a fever. You need to go to bed."

"No, I'm fine. You can't handle the sick ones alone."

"I have Thomas to help me. Now off to bed with you."

"No, really, I'll be fine."

Martha sighed as she watched her get up and start on some soup. "How long will this last?" she wondered.

By nightfall, Martha was tired, but she pressed on, determined to help. She was just taking some cool water to the boys when she heard screaming from down the hall. It came from the girls' room and it sounded like Lydia.

Mom was in with Dad and Elizabeth, so Martha set down the bucket and hurried to the girls' room and what a sight she beheld. Lydia was sitting up in bed with tears streaming down her face and she was screaming at the top of her lungs.

Martha went to her and wrapped her arms around her. "It's okay, Lydia. You're having a bad dream. Big sister's here."

Martha was terrified. She had never seen Lydia react this way to a fever before. She guessed it was probably the ferocity of the fever. "I've got to wake her up!"

Thomas stepped through the doorway and he looked stunned as well. "Thomas, get me a cup of water, please."

Thomas ran to the kitchen and got the cup of water. Martha was surprised her Mom was not there yet. But she couldn't think about that. She kept shaking Lydia to try to bring her back to her senses. All the time saying to her, "It's all right, Lydia. It's all right, Martha's here. It's all right." Sarah and Anna had awakened and had sat up in bed and looked at their sister, dumbfounded.

Thomas came back carrying the water and handed it to Martha. She took it in her hand as she continued to help Lydia calm down. Finally, the little girl started to shiver. "Martha, is that you?"

"Yes, you were having a bad dream."

"What dream? I don't remember any dream. I just woke up."

Martha was surprised that she didn't remember and replied, "Well, I'll change these sheets and get you a new nightgown. The one you're in is all sweaty."

All three girls got out of bed and huddled on the floor in a corner while Martha changed the bedding, changed Lydia into a fresh gown and tucked her sisters back into bed.

Martha took a big, deep breath as her sisters fell asleep. "Thank You, Lord, for helping me. I really was scared."

She decided to check on her Mom. It just dawned on her that she had not appeared at any point of the ordeal.

She stepped into the room to find her Mom on the bed, her face and hair drenched in sweat. She tucked another quilt around her and put a cloth to her head. Mom's eyes were rimmed with red. Martha gave her some quinine to help bring down the fever and went to check on James.

After she checked on James, she noticed that Mom was up. "How are you, Mom?"

"I'm sorry, dear, I must've fallen asleep. I can help you now."

"It's okay. Why don't you lie back down?"

"No, no, I'm okay. Thank you for offering though."

Martha recounted Lydia's bad dream to her mother and Mom apologized for not being there, then they moved on with their day.

By the next morning, Martha and Mom had given their patients the last bit of quinine. She sighed as she set the bottle on the counter.

"Thomas, do you think you can handle everyone for a bit? We're out of medicine and I think the McShire's will have some. I need to go to their place."

"Are you sure, Martha? It's been snowing all night."

"Yes, I have too. The doctor is too far to fetch. I'll be fine. I should be back in a half hour at the most."

"Okay, Martha. I don't like it though. But I guess it's our only option. Be careful!"

"I will, don't worry."

Martha slipped into her coat and scarf and stepped out to head to her friend's house. It was bitterly cold and Martha fought against the wind. She headed toward the woods, praying as she went that she would be able to find her way back with the medicine. She had brought along some ribbons to tie around the branches of trees to help her.

She had been walking for about ten minutes when she got up the big hill that separated her house from the McShire's. She narrowed her eyes, trying to see through the wind and snow. Finally, she could see a little light in a window and stumbled toward their front porch.

As she knocked, she noticed her fists were numb, so her knock couldn't be heard over the wind. She used the toe of her shoe and knocked as hard as she could. Leslie McShire opened the door and her eyes widened as she saw her neighbor. "Why, Martha, you look half frozen. Come on in and warm yourself."

Martha tried to smile, but noticed her lips were so numb that she could barely talk. She stepped into the living room and Polly looked up from her knitting and knew by the look on her face that something was wrong. "Why, Martha, what's wrong?" Martha tried to talk but her lips barely moved.

"Polly McShire, give her a chance to warm up," chuckled Mrs. McShire.

Martha stood by the fire and five minutes later she was able to speak again. "M-my f-family is sick w-with the f-flu and I-I've run out of q-q-quinine."

"Oh, you poor thing; did your whole family come down with it?"

"Yes ma'am. T-Thomas and I are the only ones left that a-aren't sick—yet."

"Well, I think we have almost a whole bottle left. And I'm coming with you to help. You and Thomas can't possibly handle all this by yourself."

"Oh, no ma'am, you might catch it. T-Thomas and I will manage just fine. Don't worry about us."

"Well, I'm afraid that I will worry about you, so I'm coming to help anyway," replied Mrs. McShire.

As Mrs. McShire put on her coat, she said to her daughter, "Polly, I have a roast in the oven for dinner. I'll probably be staying overnight, so you are the lady of the house while I'm gone."

"Yes, ma'am, I hope everyone gets better soon, Martha."

"Thanks, I would give you a hug, but I don't want to give this sickness to you."

"That's okay. Be careful!"

"We will, don't worry," assured Polly's Mom.

Thanks to Martha's markings with the ribbons, they were able to get to the house safely. They both stepped through the front door as Thomas was putting another log on the fire.

After warming up, Mrs. McShire convinced Martha and Thomas to lie down for a bit while she tended to the sick ones. And with some reluctance, Martha laid down on the couch while Thomas made himself a little floor bed.

The next day, everyone's fever had started to go down. Thankfully Martha, Thomas, and the McShire's were spared the illness, which brought a round of gratefulness to God that it didn't get any worse than it did.

Chapter 4
Blizzard

The Knight family was finally over the flu and three days later they were back to chores and school, although they were still pretty weak.

Friday morning dawned and Martha got up and did her chores, ate her breakfast, and started on the dishes. She looked out the window, expecting to see a sunny lawn and the chickens out in the barnyard, but to her utter dismay, big snow clouds were steadily approaching. She could see the snow that was falling a couple hundred yards ahead. She put the last dish in the cabinet and called her Mom. "Mom, just look at those clouds!"

Mom, who was in the living room helping Anna with her English, gave her daughter a puzzled look at the urgency of her voice. But her eyes went to the window. She saw the clouds and a hurried expression came over her face.

"Martha, go out and get your Dad. We'll have to hustle to get everything ready before the blizzard hits."

"Okay, Mom."

Martha put on her coat and scarf and ran out to the barn. "Dad, there are snow clouds in the west coming in and it looks like we'll have a blizzard. Mom told me to come get you."

Dad took a look outside and confirmed what his wife had said. "Martha, gather all the chickens into the barn where they will be safe and warm," ordered her dad as he put a horse blanket over Zoe and Vernon and patted them as he looked at the rolling clouds. Then he started to rig rope from the barn to the house.

Martha ushered the chickens into the barn and gave them some extra feed so they would settle down. Then checking on the horses before she left, barred the doors and started walking to the house, but not before she heard a voice yelling, "Martha! Martha! Can you open the door?"

She realized it was James' voice coming from inside the barn. She noticed that she had barred the doors with her brother still in it.

She hurried and unlocked the door and exclaimed, "I'm so sorry James. I didn't know you were in there."

"It's fine. I was putting away the tools, but I'm done now. Thomas has already gone to the house."

"Good." They both headed toward the house to get warm. As she stepped in the door, her mother asked her to go down to the cellar and gather some of the canned vegetables that they had picked from earlier in the fall.

So she re-buttoned her coat and went down to the cellar. She gathered all the preserves she could carry in a bag, but before she left, she heard a purring noise. She turned to the left and saw her kitten, Jubilee, in the corner, licking her paw.

Martha stared at her. "How did you ever get

in here? I guess probably when Mom came down to get something. You'd better come on in the house before you freeze. I'll give you some milk."

The cat stormed out the door and was waiting for her when she came to the back porch. "Jubilee, I declare, I'll never know how you get yourself in such fixes." And with that, she and the cat went into the house to finally warm up.

That night, the boys, Martha, and their parents were sitting around the fire. Martha was reading a book and the boys were finishing up some history.

"I sure hope this storm doesn't get too bad." exclaimed Mom.

"Me too," Dad agreed.

"Hopefully it won't last too long. It came very quickly. I hope our friends are okay."

"I'm sure they are. They're wise people."

"You're right," she sighed and laid her head on her husband's shoulder.

Ten minutes went by and suddenly they heard a scream from upstairs.

"It must be Lydia," started Martha, hurrying up the stairs.

Lydia still struggled with having nightmares. Martha and Mom hurried upstairs and they started shaking her to wake her up.

"Lydia, Lydia! Wake up darling. You're just having a bad dream. Everything's all right. Wake up," said Mom soothingly, still shaking her.

"Martha, get me a cup of water, please," Mom asked.

"Yes, Mom," Martha fetched the cup and hurried back upstairs. But as she got to the door, Lydia wasn't screaming anymore. There were tear stains on her face.

"It's all over now and I'll sit here with you till you fall asleep."

"Thanks, Mommy. May I have a drink of water?"

"Yes, you may."

Martha handed her mother the cup and Lydia sipped from it, laid her head on her pillow and closed her eyes.

Martha woke the next morning and helped get breakfast on the table. Lydia was fine. She was her normal, cheerful self and she was bouncing around the kitchen while Martha was making pancakes.

"Calm down, Lydia," commanded her sister playfully.

"But I'm hungry and I can't wait to have some of your delicious pancakes."

"I know, but I think you could help Sarah and Anna set the table."

"All right," agreed Lydia, gathering the silverware on the counter and applying her hands to work.

About twenty minutes later the whole family sat down to breakfast and Dad said the blessing. As they were putting the delicious pancakes on their plates, Dad began to speak. "Today, since the snow is still blowing hard, I want to have a cleanup day. So I'm going to assign some chores for each of you. Boys, we are going to go out to the barn and sort all the tools and just clean up. Girls, your mother will tell you what she wants you to do," Dad finished and looked toward his wife.

"Martha, I want you to clean the living room thoroughly. Lydia and Anna, you will sort out your closet, while Sarah will clean and dust the room. That should last you girls all morning. I'm going to be baking this morning and then I'll need Martha's help cleaning up the kitchen."

"Okay, since everyone has finished their pancakes, why don't Martha and Sarah do the cleanup?"

The girls got up and started clearing the table.

Martha was cleaning up in the kitchen after lunch and she looked out the window as she was washing the dishes. She hoped that Polly and her family were well and all her friends. "I wonder if there will be any damage? I surely hope not."

Martha put the last dish away and as the snow continued to fall, she sighed and wondered how long this winter would last.

Two days later, the snow had stopped and Martha was now stumbling to the barn in snow that was half-way up to her waist. It was Saturday and Martha was glad to be outdoors again, even though it was twenty-three degrees outside. She got tired about halfway there, but she gave a little extra effort and finally reached the barn door and fell to her knees at the effort to pull open the door. "Good morning!"

"Good morning, Martha. Did you sleep well?" asked Dad, who was milking Cassie.

"I slept fine. Although Lydia woke up with a nightmare once, but thankfully it wasn't as bad as all the others she's had."

"Well, I'm sorry she woke you up, but hopefully that's a sign that the dreams are subsiding."

"I sure hope so."

Martha set to work feeding the chickens and then groomed Zoe and Vernon. "It sure is cold outside; I'm glad the snow has stopped. This was a really early blizzard; we usually get them in January."

"Yes, it is unusually early," agreed Dad.

"Hey Martha," started James, who had just climbed down from the loft. "Who was the robber who stole your soap?"

Martha, realizing this was a joke, replied, "I don't know. Who stole the soap?"

"A ROBBER ducky!"

"Oh, a robber ducky—a rubber ducky. That's funny."

"Thanks. I learned it from Bruce Gates."

"Well, how many jokes does he know so I can be watching out for more?" Martha teased.

"Very funny," and he turned and walked out the side door of the barn.
Martha finished up her barn chores and headed to the house to warm up. "See you at breakfast, Dad."

"See you later," he called, looking over his shoulder.

After devotions, Dad announced that they would be going to the Bear family's house to see if they needed any help cleaning up after the blizzard.

They would take food, in case they didn't have enough, and offer their help.

The Bear family had just recently moved to Montana from Idaho in late November. The Knight family hadn't met them yet and Martha was anxious to meet them.

"I hope they have children. Maybe they'll have a girl my age!" exclaimed Martha excitedly.

"Martha, would you please hurry and get Elizabeth ready? I have the food just about packed and ready to load into the wagon." prodded Mom.

"Sure, Mom. Sorry. I guess I'm just excited."

"It's okay, honey. I'm excited, too," answered Mom.

Martha finished getting her sister ready and went outside, put her in the back of the wagon, climbed in herself and sat beside her. Two minutes later, the wagon jolted forward and off they went.

About thirty minutes later, the Knight family pulled into a nice grove of trees that led up to the Bear's front door. The porch was surrounded by flowers and Martha thought it looked like a very nice place. It could use a bit of cleaning up, though. The porch steps needed a new coat of paint and a tree had fallen about ten feet from the barn because of the blizzard.

Dad stopped the wagon and put the brake on and called, "Anybody home?"

A man about the age of fifty stepped out of the house with a lady, who Martha guessed to be his wife.

"Hello; are we neighbors?" asked Mr. Bear.

"I suppose we are. We live about thirty minutes west from here as the crow flies; we're the Knight family. This is my wife, Rosemary, and these are my children." Dad introduced them each in turn by their age and each was polite and said hello.

"Well, why don't you come in? I just brewed up some coffee and you're welcome to it," suggested Mrs. Bear.

Once they had stepped through the front door, Mr. Bear introduced themselves. After calling for his children, they all bounded in and stared wide eyed at the strangers.

"I'm Daniel Bear, and this is my wife, Erin, and my children: Francesca, who's thirteen, Billy who's ten, and my youngest is Jenny and she's seven. Children, say hello to the Knight family."

The children said a polite, but very quiet hello and Jenny hid behind her mother's skirt. "Come on, Jenny," prodded her mother, pulling her daughter out. "They don't bite."

"Mommy," started Sarah, "what does Mrs. Bear mean by we don't bite? We aren't bugs."

"I'll explain later, honey," said Mom, whispering in her ear, trying to keep from chuckling.

"Well, come on in and get warmed up. My wife will get you grownups some coffee and the younger ones can have some warm hot chocolate."

"That would be great. Our real reason for coming is to see if you needed any help cleaning up from the blizzard." Dad added.

"Well, that's right kind of you. There has been a tree that has fallen and Billy and I could use your help chopping it up for firewood. We're mighty obliged." Daniel Bear smiled warmly.
"All right, that'll be fine," agreed Dad.

Meanwhile, Martha walked up to Francesca and extended her hand to shake it, but Francesca's hand didn't move from behind her back. Martha let her hand drop and decided that she must be shy. "Hi. I'm Martha Knight. It seems that we're both the same age. When's your birthday?"

"June 8th," she replied shortly and went to help her Mom in the kitchen.

Martha stared after her in utter astonishment. She would get in trouble if she talked that way. But she just followed her and decided to try again. "Do you like to play games?"

"Sure, they're okay," replied Francesca.

"Have you ever played cat's cradle before?"

"Of course!" she exclaimed irritatingly. "Everyone knows that game, and I think that it's quite a boring and babyish game. I prefer to read."

"I love to read, too. I'm currently reading a book named *Amelia*. It's really good and maybe you would want to borrow it sometime?"

"I've already read that book. It was okay."

Martha was very puzzled with Francesca's behavior, but tried to keep up the conversation. "Are you homeschooled?"

"No, I go to your little quaint school. I haven't seen you there before, though."

"Well, I haven't been there. I'm homeschooled."

"How can you stand that? However do you meet new friends? I think I'd DIE if I didn't go to school."

"It's actually quite fun being homeschooled and I have several friends at church. I'm sure you'll like them when you come to church this week."

"Oh, church is such a bore, sitting there for hours on end, hearing the old preacher talk and talk and TALK!"

Martha was shocked to hear her talk this way. "Well, I enjoy church a lot. I get to learn from God's Word and we all sing songs to Him. I love Sundays."

"Humph. I sure don't," and she stalked off with her cup of hot chocolate.

Martha just stared at her.

After they finished their hot drinks, the boys went out to start chopping at the fallen oak tree.

Meanwhile the girls were going to be stacking the wood the boys chopped alongside the house.

Mrs. Bear set Jenny and Anna to dusting the sitting room and the living room. Lydia and Sarah were instructed to work on arranging a bowl of buttons and separating them by color. Mom was going to help Mrs. Bear with mopping the kitchen floor, and Martha and Francesca started on stacking the first load of wood.

They wrapped up in their warmest clothing and Francesca got gloves from their barn and they both set to work. Martha thought this would be a good time to witness to her.

"Are you excited about Christmas coming up?"

"Yeah, I'm really hoping to get some new cloth to make a dress. It was really pretty, but also kind of expensive. But I surely do hope I get it."

Martha wasn't surprised to hear this from their earlier conversation.

"Francesca, do you know the real meaning of Christmas?"

"Yeah, kinda; wasn't a baby born that day, or something like that?"

Martha thought to herself, *Wow, she doesn't even know much about the true meaning of Christmas.* But she replied, "Yes, a baby was born that night. His name was Jesus. Actually, scholars believe he was born sometime in the spring, but

December 25ᵗʰ is just the day we chose to celebrate it. He was the promised baby that would crush the enemy, Satan's, head."

"How was that?"

"Well, I'm sure you've heard the story of Adam and Eve, right?"

"Yeah, I've heard that story at least a dozen times," she replied.

"Well, God promised that a Deliverer would come and save His people from Satan's bondage. Do you know what He did?"

"Something about dying for somebody....I think."

"He came to this earth to live among us, a sinful and wicked people, and was beaten, and nailed to a cross for our sins."

"Why would He do a thing like that?"

"Because He loved us SO much! John 3:16 says: *'For God so loved the world that He gave His only begotten Son, that whoever believes in Him should not perish but have everlasting life.'* He died so that we could be free and go to Heaven if we receive His gift."

"What gift?"

"God says in His Word that the 'wages of sin is death, but the GIFT of God is eternal life through Christ Jesus our Lord.'"

"What crime have I done? I'm a pretty good person."

"That's what the devil wants us to think, but we are just as guilty as the greatest sinners. If we break even one commandment, it is as if we've broken all TEN!"

"Oh, well..., I..I'm not sure if I'm ready for all that stuff. I'm kinda happy the way I am. I like my school, my friends back home. I want everything to stay the way it is."

"I'll be praying for you, Francesca."

"Well, I didn't ask for any of your prayers! I don't need them! I'm going to get a drink," and she stomped off.

Martha looked after her in sad dismay and decided she needed to have a long talk with her Mom when they got home.

About three and a half hours later, the Knight family was home again. The sun was high in the sky as the boys put up the horses.

Martha went to her room, put her bonnet away and sighed; Francesca wasn't what she thought she would be. She decided to see if her Mom was free so she could talk to her.

"Mom? Are you free for a moment?" asked Martha, as she stepped into the living room where she found Mom helping Lydia with her numbers.

"Yes, Martha," she whispered something in her younger daughter's ear; Lydia nodded and ran off to find Sarah.

"Yes, Martha, is something wrong?"

"No; not exactly, well, you see. Francesca was very short with me, and also kind of mean. I was trying to witness to her and everything seemed to be going well. She seemed willing and eager to listen, but then she threw the statement that she thought she was a 'pretty good person,' and I replied that we are all sinners and I explained that breaking one law, was like breaking all of them, and she turned around and mocked me."

"I'm sorry, Martha. I was talking to her mother today and some of the things she said were questionable. I don't think they go to church regularly, so I was trying to witness to her too, but I don't think she got it."
"I know, Mom, but at least she wasn't down right mean as Francesca was. Mom, you don't know how short she was with me. I was trying to be friendly, but..."

"I know, honey. Sometimes God puts people in our lives and we don't know why He put them there. But really, the best thing I can do for them is to pray. It helps me a lot. I ask Him to help me to love them as He would. Not as I would want to."

"Thanks, Mom. I'll begin praying for her. I'll put her on my prayer list."

"That's a good idea, honey. Right now, I need to get supper started and I think you have an essay to write, if I am correct?"

"Yes, ma'am, I'll go and get started on it." Martha started upstairs to her room, but turned back around when she heard her mother's voice.

"Martha, I'm proud of you."

"Thanks."

Sunday morning dawned and Martha got up and wondered if the Bear family would be at church today. "Well, I shouldn't be thinking about that right now. I'd better get the girls and myself down to help with breakfast."

She woke her sisters and helped them dress and do their hair. After pinning Elizabeth's curly brown hair back in a barrette, she carried her on her hip, with her three other sisters in tow, and went down to the kitchen. She could already smell the eggs and ham.

Her mother greeted her pleasantly. Martha put Elizabeth in her high chair and fed her the oatmeal that Mom had just finished making for her.

Anna and Lydia were talking amongst themselves while setting the table, but Sarah, who had her chin in her hand, gazed with downcast eyes at the table.

"What's the matter, Sarah?"

"Nothing."

"Well, there must be something if you keep that frown on your face."

"Well, Jenny Bear kept 'noring me yesterday. All her attention was on Anna and Lydia. I don't think she likes me because I'm too little."

"You mean 'ignoring'?"

"Yes."

"Well, I'm sorry about that. I'm not sure why she's ignoring you, but would you like to pray for her right now? That would be the best thing to do."

"Sure."

Martha held out her hands and her sister's went into them. She led them in a short prayer. "Dear Father in Heaven, Sarah has met a new girl, and I know You know her name. She is not acting very nice toward Sarah and we ask You to change her heart. Please help her to be nice and please help Sarah to be patient and kind. In Your Son's most Holy Name, amen."

"I feel better already. Thank you Martha."

"You're welcome. Now help Mom carry drinks to the table while I finish feeding Elizabeth her breakfast."

About an hour and a half later, the Knight family arrived at church and Martha carried their hymnals with Elizabeth hanging onto her skirt and walking wobbly toward the church.
"Good morning, Martha. How are you this morning?" asked Mrs. Hard, a neighbor of theirs.

"I'm doing very well; how is your arthritis?"

"Oh, it's not the best, but it's better now than it has been. Praise the Lord."

"Well, I'll be praying for you."

"Thank you, I'd appreciate it very much; I see your baby sister has started walkin'."

"Yes. Would you like to hold her? She loves you."

"Yes," and she started cooing to Elizabeth

and the baby held her arms out and walked three very wobbly steps toward her and fell into her arms.

Martha walked into the church and undid her wraps and hung them on a peg by the door. She took the hymnals to their pew and set the books down. She scanned the room for her friends and was heartened and dismayed at the same time as she saw Francesca Bear in the corner looking very bored and shy. *Lord, help me to witness.*

She walked over to where she was standing and said, "Hello, Francesca. How are you this lovely morning?"

"Fine, I guess."

"I don't see any of my other friends here yet, but when they get here, I'll introduce them to you."

"Okay, that'll be fine."

About five minutes later, Cathryn and Timothy Williams stepped through the door. Cathryn was carrying Kathy, their baby sister, with her other siblings close behind.

Martha gave her a look that said, "Come on over here", and after she settled Kathy in Rose's arms, Cathryn walked over and gave Francesca a smile as she extended her hand. "Hi. I'm Cathryn Williams. What's yours?"

"Francesca Bear."

"It's nice to meet you. Hello, Martha. How's your week been?"

"Good, how about yours?"

"Mine was fine."

"Are you homeschooled, too?! I haven't seen you in school this week," asked Francesca harshly.

Cathryn gave Martha a look that asked her "why did she say 'too'"?

But she turned to her and replied that yes she was and then went on and asked her what subject she liked best.

A few minutes later, Polly McShire, along with Cara and Mary Poltor, joined their small group and another round of introductions went around. After they all started talking about school and general stuff, Francesca exclaimed rudely, "You don't mean to tell me that you all are homeschooled? Is there anybody here that isn't?"

"Well, actually, you are the first," Martha replied politely, although she was boiling mad inside, but she tried to remain patient and kind.

Just then, Pastor Share started the service, breaking up the uncomfortable silence. As Martha was walking back to her pew with Mary and Cara Poltor, Mary whispered in her ear before departing, "Boy, that girl has some nerve."

Martha just nodded in assent and tried to keep from laughing out loud.

After the service was concluded, the girls gathered in a corner to chat. Martha tried to get Francesca to participate in the conversation, but mostly, she just stood there with a pout on her face. Finally, it was time for lunch, and the girls filled their plates and went to sit down at a table the boys had set up.

As Martha was finishing a conversation with Polly, Jenny Bear, came up to her sister and asked, "Franny, please get me some more water from the pitcher. Mommy said for me to ask you. She's afraid I'll break the pitcher."

"Oh, Jenny, can't you get Billy?"

"No. Mommy told me to get you."

"Okay, okay, I'll get you your water." She backed her chair out irritatingly and grabbed her sister by the hand and practically dragged her to the water. Rose looked wide eyed and exclaimed, "I'd get in trouble if I acted that way to my siblings—and I wouldn't like to treat my siblings that way, either." Everyone was equally shocked at their new friend's attitude.

When she finally came back to the table, she sat down hard and proclaimed, "Little sisters are always such a bother."

"No," Martha contradicted. "I don't think they are. I think they are a blessing. I'll be praying for you to see your siblings in a different light. I'm very sorry you happen to feel that way toward your own sister. The Bible says to love one another and that's what I try to do and I hope my actions are pleasing to my Father in Heaven."

Francesca just pouted and went back to her lunch. Under the table, Cara, who was sitting beside her, gave her hand a pat as if saying "good job". Martha smiled her thanks and went back to her meal.

That night, Martha got ready for bed and read a chapter in her Bible and then wrote in her diary.

December 20ᵗʰ, 1930

Dear God,

I have met a certain young lady by the name of Miss Francesca Bear. She is not the nicest of persons I have ever met. She was very rude to everyone at church today. Oh, she had the decency to be nice to the adults and hold her tongue, but around us, she just ran her tongue and just said the rudest things. I tried to look at her in a different light as Mom has taught me to do since I was a small child, but this time, it hasn't worked very well. Lord, please help me to see her in a different way and take this dislike for her away. Help me to see her and love her like You would, Lord.

Love, Your Daughter,

Martha Rosemary Knight.

Chapter 5
Christmas

Wednesday, December 23rd, two days before Christmas, Martha was sitting by the fire reading to her sisters the story of Jesus feeding the five thousand when there was a knock at the door.

Mom came down from being upstairs where she had been changing Elizabeth's diaper and answered the door. Martha continued reading, but her ears were pricked.

"Oh, hello Erin, how are you?"

"We're well; how about you?"

"We're doing great. Come on in from the cold."

"Thank you. The girls and I made you some cookies as a thank you for helping us with the work that Friday after the blizzard. We really did appreciate it."

Martha looked up to see Mrs. Bear, Francesca, and Jenny. Martha prayed for the Lord to give her patience and told her sisters that she would finish their story later.

Closing the Bible and laying it on the side table, Martha went over to Francesca and touched her shoulder to get her attention. "Why don't you come with me to the kitchen? I need to get started with lunch, and I could use your help."

"All right," replied Francesca, following Martha to the kitchen where she gathered up some carrots and potatoes and let Francesca peel the vegetables while she boiled some water. "So, how's your week been so far?"

"So-so. I miss my friends a lot."

"I know it's really hard to make new friends and I hope we'll become fast friends soon."

"Oh, I don't know about that. I don't think anyone could replace my best friend, Sally Watson."

"Is she your age?"

"Yes, I'm about a week younger than her."

"Well, I hope you get to see her again soon."

"Uh-huh."

Silence came over the two and all that was heard was the chopping of the knife. "I'm done," exclaimed Francesca.

"Okay, if you'll come and dump those in this pot of water, I'll get the salt, pepper and thyme to season it."

Francesca slid the vegetables into the pot and then took a seat at the table and sighed.

"Has it been hard on you since you moved away?"

"Yes, it has. I don't know why we moved away. I was fine where I was."

"A lot of times, I don't understand why God lets things happen the way they do, but I know He can be trusted."

"I'm not really sure about that right now. How can He be trusted when He takes away everything that I've ever known?"

"I don't know why He moved you away from your friends, but I do know that He cares for you very much."

"Yeah, well, I don't want to talk about it," and she stalked off toward the living room.

Later, at supper, as everyone was finishing up eating, Mom began, "Peter, I invited the Bear family to come and spend Christmas with us. I invited them to come Christmas Eve and spend the night and spend Christmas day. I knew that I spoke for both of us. I think it would be a good time to witness to them."

"You did right, Honey, thank you. Children,

your mother and I have an announcement to make. We have invited the Bear family to come and spend Christmas with us." He went over the details and afterwards everyone added his or her own feelings about it.

"I think it's a great idea. Billy is fun to be with," exclaimed James and Thomas nodded his approval.

The girls agreed that it would be fun, but Martha didn't think she would have that much fun with Francesca, but looked forward to witnessing to her. *Lord, I'm not the most happy about the plan, but wouldn't it be wonderful if they became Christians on Christmas?* Martha prayed.

A few minutes later, Martha and Mom got up to clear the table.

Christmas Eve morning arrived and Martha was up early to get started with the cleaning. She quickly dressed and bundled up and went out to the barn to do her morning chores.

After grooming the horses and feeding the chickens, she headed back to the house to help her Mom get started on breakfast. On her way to the house she got an arm load of wood and dumped it into the wood box.

"Mom, I'm ready to help with breakfast; is there anything I can do?"

"Actually, Martha, I'm fine here. Would you go and get Elizabeth dressed? I think I hear your sisters talking while they dress, so I know they're awake."

"Sure Mom. I'd be happy to."

"Thank you, dear."

Martha hurried up the stairs and greeted her sisters with a jolly, "Merry Christmas!" She went over to her sister's crib and lifted her out and placed her on the bed so she could change her diaper and dress her.

Before long, she and the others were all trooping down to the breakfast table where Dad had just seated his wife and the boys were just sitting down. Martha put Elizabeth in her high chair beside Mom and took her place in between Sarah and Anna.

Dad bowed his head to pray.

"Dear Heavenly Father, thank You for blessing us with another year. Thank You for sending us Your only Son to this sinful earth to die for our sins. Please help us to be gratcful for all You have blessed us with. In Jesus' Name we pray, amen."

Everyone feasted on the pancakes and bacon Mom had prepared for them. After the dishes were done, everyone trooped into the living room for family morning devotions. They were reading from Job and after their chapter and prayer, everyone decided on what chores they wanted to cover. After a quick hymn to wrap everything up, all got to work at their assigned chores, even Elizabeth put the toys that were in her room away in the toy basket, which Mom praised her for.

Martha's assigned chores were to:

Sweep girls', boys' and the living room.
Dust living room.
Put new sheets on the beds.
Make sure there is enough oil in the lamps.

Martha decided to start with the bed sheets, so after getting the sheets from the linen closet, she ripped off all the old sheets, put the clean ones on and neatly made them up again; making them look pretty with the quilts. Looking at the two beds with satisfaction, she hurried to do the dusting.

She coughed up a storm as all the dust spread everywhere. "Somebody's been neglecting their job of dusting, looks like this desk hasn't been dusted for a couple of weeks."

The dusting job was normally Sarah's job, but today Martha got the chore. She went in search of her mother and found her scrubbing the kitchen floor. "Mom, I think Sarah has been neglecting her job as duster. There was at least an inch of dust on the piano and side table."

"Thank you, Martha. But do you remember our rule about not tale bearing?"

"Oh, I guess I didn't think about that. I'm sorry."

"It's okay, you just made a mistake. Here. I'll take the duster for you and if you see Sarah, please send her to me."

"Yes, ma'am," replied Martha, reproving herself of tale bearing and deciding to do better.

Lunch was a bit later than usual, and everyone seemed to be in a hurry to eat; after doing the dishes, Mom, Martha, and now Anna, who was old enough to help, started cooking the pies.

The turkey would wait for the early morning where Mom would get up at four a.m. to get everything set for Christmas and get a few more last minute presents wrapped.

Martha started peeling the last bag of apples that they would have for that winter, while Anna chopped them with the knife and Mom prepared the dough for the pie crust. "I'm really going to savor and enjoy these apple pies since they'll be the last ones we'll have until next summer," exclaimed

Anna with a little sigh.

"Yes, I know. We'll all be enjoying them," replied Martha, looking at the almost full bowl of apple peelings. "Come to think of it, we really shouldn't be wasting any of these apple shavings. They still have some apple on them where I accidentally didn't cut close enough to the peeling; I have an excellent idea. What if we dipped them in honey? We still have five jars of honey left from the store."

"That's a great idea, Martha. I can drizzle some sugar and cinnamon over them to give them extra flavor," exclaimed Mom.

"Thanks. I've finished peeling these apples and I'll put a towel over the bowl and put them in the ice box so they'll stay fresh."

By four o'clock, everything was ready for their visitors and the house had a pleasant aroma of baking pies. There were three apple pies, and Mom had made a delicious stew. So they would have a grand feast of stew and apple pie.

At six o'clock sharp, there was a loud rap at the door and Dad stood up from his place at the kitchen table, walked over to the door and opened it. "Hello, Bear family. Come on in and make yourselves comfortable. James and Thomas, help them with their stuff, please."

Thomas and James came forward and helped them with their luggage. They were soon seated in the living room. Mrs. Bear went to the kitchen to help the girls who were working at setting the table for supper.

Martha wondered why Francesca wasn't right behind Mrs. Bear and Jenny. She looked toward the kitchen entrance and still no Francesca. Martha shrugged her shoulders and got back to work at setting the table.

About ten minutes later, Mom came into the living room and called everyone to supper. Daniel Bear was talking to Dad, and James and Thomas were joking around with Billy.

Martha noticed Francesca, who had been standing in a dark corner with a lonely look on her face. Martha pitied her and went over and put an arm around her shoulder. "Come on, we can sit together."

"Okay," said Francesca quietly.

Dad bowed his head to pray and everyone followed his lead. "Dear Father in Heaven, thank You so much for seeing us through another joyous year. Thank You for blessing us with so many things, even though we do not deserve it. Please help us to honor and glorify You this Christmas season. We love You. In Jesus Name we pray, amen."

"Let's eat!" exclaimed Dad and he passed around the bowl of stew, bread and butter and everyone ate heartily; thankful for what they had.

Mr. Bear had started a conversation on what crops he was going to grow next spring and Mom started a conversation with Mrs. Bear. Everyone was in jolly spirits.

"So, Francesca, do you feel excited?" questioned Martha.

"Yeah, I guess," she replied.

"Me too! I can't wait to read the Christmas story tonight!"

"Oh, yeah.... me too."

After supper was finished, Martha and Anna did the dishes while everyone else adjourned to the living room.

It did not take long to do the dishes and when Anna and Martha were finished, they joined the others in the living room where Dad began to hand out the hymnals.

"It is tradition in our house to read the Christmas story of how the Lord Jesus came to earth as a little baby, to be born in this world, and God's plan for redemption."
"Yes, that's fine. I would love to see how you

celebrate Christmas," Mr. Bear asserted.

"Okay, why don't we sing 'Come Thou Long Expected Jesus'? That's a popular one I think everyone knows."

Everyone began the hymn:

Come, Thou long expected Jesus, Born to set Thy people free.
From our fears and sins release us; Let us find our rest in Thee.
Israel's Strength and Consolation, Hope of all the earth Thou art;
Dear Desire of every nation, Joy of every longing heart.

Born Thy people to deliver, Born a Child and yet a King,
Born to reign in us forever, Now Thy gracious kingdom bring.
By Thine own eternal Spirit, Rule in all our hearts alone;
By Thine all sufficient merit, Raise us to Thy glorious throne.

"That was great, everyone. Now let's open our Bibles to Luke 2:4-40"

"And Joseph also went up from Galilee, out of the city of Nazareth, into Judaea, unto the city of David, which is called Bethlehem; (because he was of the house and lineage of David:) To be

taxed with Mary his espoused wife, being great with child. And so it was, that, while they were there, the days were accomplished that she should be delivered. And she brought forth her firstborn son, and wrapped him in swaddling clothes, and laid him in a manger; because there was no room for them in the inn..."

Dad closed the Bible and said, "Well, that's the story of how our Savior came to earth as a baby. Now, let's sing 'Silent Night'."

Silent night, holy night, All is calm, all is bright
Round yon virgin mother and Child. Holy Infant so tender and mild,
Sleep in heavenly peace, Sleep in heavenly peace.
Silent night, holy night, Shepherds quake at the sight.
Glories stream from heaven a far; Heavenly hosts sing alleluia.
Christ the Savior is born! Christ the Savior is born!

For the next hour the Bear and Knight Family sang songs. They sang: "Good Christian Men Rejoice," "Angels We Have Heard on High," "Joy to the World" and "O, Little Town of Bethlehem" and many others that before they knew it, it was time for bed.

Francesca helped Martha get the younger ones to bed and then they trooped downstairs,

Martha with her Bible in her hand and Francesca with a book.

The two girls were allowed to stay up till ten o'clock that night. So they sat by the fire, their shawls wrapped around their shoulders and their heads bent in reading before them.

Martha thought that this would be a good time to witness to her new friend. She began with: "Francesca, have you ever thought of where you're going when you die?"

"No, not really, I never found it important to think about."

"Francesca, it is VERY important. God loves you and wants to take you to heaven to live with Him someday in the future. Whether He comes while we are living, or we die and we go to be with Him. But you must have asked Him into your heart."

Martha continued, "So we are left with a choice: to live eternity with Him forever, or the alternative, an eternity in Hell. Which will you choose? I want to someday live with Him in Heaven. I can't wait to sit on His lap and tell Him everything and see Him face to face."

"I don't know. I guess I need more time to think about it."

Martha decided to drop the subject and opened her Bible again to read in Psalms. At nine forty-five, they said goodnight to their parents who were talking nearby, and hurried upstairs and got ready for bed.

Anna, Lydia, and Sarah were sharing a bed and Jenny and Francesca were sharing the other while Martha had made a floor bed made of quilts. Once she said her prayers and with a special prayer offered up to heaven for the saving of her new, hurting friend, she drifted off to a peaceful sleep.

Francesca, you could say, didn't have as peaceful a sleep as her newly found friend. She heard a Voice calling for her come to Him for the rest, joy and peace she was looking for, but she didn't know who the voice was.

This was a Francesca who was insecure and was trying to search for the right way. But inside that defiant heart, there was a glimmer of hope that felt that she would eventually find what she was looking for.

Christmas morning, Martha awoke to the sound of Elizabeth thumping her legs on her bed.

Martha got up from her floor bed and looked out the window. *It must be seven o'clock already.* Martha turned to get Elizabeth dressed and as she did, she called out, "Time to get up. Today is the day the Lord has made. Let us rejoice and be glad in it, Merry Christmas!"

Sarah jerked up in bed, "Is it really Christmas?" She looked out the window and saw all the snow, "Yes, must be." She hopped out of bed and exclaimed to Jenny and her sisters: "Hurry, get dressed. It's Christmas morning!"

Anna yawned and sat up in bed. "I can already smell the pancakes. Come on Sarah and Lydia, I'll help you get dressed."

Francesca, who had supposedly not awakened with all the joyful exclamations, still lay on her back, sleeping soundly. Elizabeth, who was now dressed, went over to Francesca and patted her cheeks and started her babbling again.

Francesca woke up with a start and to her surprise a small face with curly brown hair was nose-to-nose with her. She realized it was just Elizabeth and tried to push her away. Martha put a hand on her sister's shoulder and said, "Come on, Elizabeth, leave Francesca alone."

Martha and Francesca dressed, each behind a curtain that Martha's parents had put up so each of the girls could get dressed in privacy.

After they were done refreshing themselves, Francesca and Jenny and Martha's sisters trooped downstairs. Anna was almost out the door when her sister called her back. "Anna, can I speak with you please, for a moment?"

"Sure." She came over to stand at Martha's side and pinched Elizabeth's cheek, who was happily satisfied on Martha's hip. "Anna, Sarah was talking with me a few days ago and said that Jenny had been ignoring her because she was too little. Is that true?"

"Let me think. I haven't been paying much attention to it. But now that you mention it, Sarah did seem to be left out in a lot of things Jenny and Lydia and I were playing. Am I in trouble?"

"Oh no, I was just curious. Would you please make sure Sarah gets to play with you, and just keep an eye on her for me? I will as well, but I can't be watching her all of the time. I'd really appreciate it."

"Sure, I'd be happy to."

"Thanks; now let's go down to breakfast. I can hear the others sitting down to eat." Grabbing her sister's hand, they all went down to have their Christmas breakfast.

It was a delicious breakfast and everyone enjoyed it thoroughly. Mom insisted that Martha and Lydia, who had clean up duty, put the dishes in the sink and they would do them later.

Everyone went in the living room and sat

down at their assigned places and the parents started handing out gifts. Martha helped Elizabeth open hers and in the small package were some new mittens. Elizabeth stared wide eyed at them. She touched them softly. She couldn't believe they were actually hers. Martha set the mittens aside which would be Elizabeth's pile and opened a gift of hers.

Martha carefully tore away the wrapping paper and saw a new sweater that her Mom had made. "Thank you, Mom. I love it!"

"You're welcome."

Martha set the gift away, thankful for the warm clothing and watched the others open their gifts and waited for another one to come to her.

Thomas was really happy with some new shoes, and James was just thrilled with a new scarf. His old one was worn out and he heartily thanked Martha, who had made it for him.

Martha was warmed inside that she was able to please her brother. Anna, who had just opened a package, discovered a doll. She smiled with delight and exclaimed, "Why, where did you get it? It's beautiful! I think I'll name her Faith."

"That's a good name," replied Mom who was smiling at her enjoyment.

Sarah and Lydia both got some new pencils and a drawing book, with which they were pleased. Dad and Mom both got scarves and mittens that Anna and Martha had worked hard on.

Dad had given his bride some new cloth to make a dress out of and Mom had given her groom some new hankies with his initials on them.

Francesca had indeed gotten the material she had wanted and thanked her parents for it. Billy had gotten some new ice skates, which he was showing off to Thomas and James.

Jenny got a new play tea set which she and Anna had already started playing with, with their dolls.

Martha looked around, but didn't see any more gifts under the tree. Jubilee, who had come and put herself in Martha's lap, was purring contentedly and was taking a little nap, but Martha was looking around. Was the sweater the only gift she was going to get? But then she chided herself on thinking of that. *I shouldn't be so ungrateful. There are many children in the world that don't even get one present. Lord, help me to stay content.*

"Martha, is that the only present you got?" asked Francesca curiously.

Martha's face turned pink, but replied

proudly. "Yes, it is. Isn't this sweater beautiful?" She tried to satisfy herself with looking and touching the soft yarn and watching the others play with their gifts.

What she didn't know was that her parents had watched the whole conversation and they shared between themselves a look that read that they were proud of their daughter for being grateful.

Martha helped Elizabeth build a house of blocks with the new building blocks she had received. Then she went over and watched Anna and Jenny playing tea party and played with them awhile to keep herself from her previous feelings. She then watched Sarah and Lydia draw and then before she knew it, it was time to set the table for the Christmas lunch.

There were pies that they had baked the day before and there was the turkey and dressing and before long they had all the good food on the table.

Dad said the blessing, "Dear Jesus, thank You SO much for coming to this earth as a baby to die on a cross in our place. Thank You for all this good food which You have blessed us with. Please help us to be thankful for it. Amen."

Everyone started eating and all the children were talking of their new gifts and how they were going to enjoy them. Francesca began explaining about all the details she was going to make on her new dress and Martha listened patiently. But with all the sharing, she was facing more of an ungrateful spirit and she prayed more than once to be grateful for what she had and finally thought of what she was thankful for: she had her friends, her family and also Jubilee. And suddenly, all that ungratefulness just went away. She thanked the Lord and hurried to help Mom put the dishes in the sink.

They once again adjourned to the living room and started to sing hymns and before they knew it, it was time for the Bear family to head back home.

The Knight family helped them get loaded and Mom heated up several potatoes to help heat their hands on the drive home. About a half hour of loading up, they were gone and the Knight family set to work cleaning up the house after the fun time.

The younger girls went upstairs to clean their room and the boys, theirs. Martha and Mom did the dishes and Martha put some biscuits in the oven for a light supper. After the table and counter and all the dishes were done, she went to the living room to read.

After a light supper that night, and after they had finished with devotions, they sat around the fire, the younger ones playing with their toys and the older ones reading.

By eight o'clock, Dad and the boys went out to the barn to do the evening chores while Mom and Martha put the other ones to bed.

After that was done, Martha sat down to read in her Bible. As the clock struck nine, Martha yawned and stood up, told her parents good night and was about to leave the room when Dad called her back, "Martha, come here."

"Yes?" she came over and stood by him.

"Come, sit," and he patted his knee in indication for her to sit there. After being seated upon his knee, she asked, "What is it, Dad? Did I do something wrong?"

"No, dear, your mother and I heard the conversation between Francesca and yourself, and we are proud of our daughter in being grateful for what she has."

"Thanks, Dad."

"Was it hard for you?"

"Yes, it was. But I remembered that a lot of children don't get any presents at all."

"Yes, and most of all, we are proud that you are trying to witness to her. We have seen that Francesca isn't the nicest of people and we are proud of you."

"Thanks," she replied the least bit embarrassed.

"We also have one more gift for you." He pulled a small package out of his pocket and placed it in her hand. "This is just a little gift saying how proud we are of you."

Martha opened the box and to her delight saw that it was a necklace with a cross on it. The cross was gold colored and Martha gazed at it with pleasure. "Thank you so much," and she hugged both parents. "It's the greatest gift I've ever received....except the gift of my salvation."

"Yes, the gift of salvation is much greater. Now, off to bed with you."

"Thank you ever so much. Goodnight!" Martha went upstairs to bed thinking that this was the best Christmas she had ever had.

Chapter 6
A New Year and a Joyous Event

New Year's Eve came round and the Knight family was having the McShire family over for dinner and they were staying till midnight.

Martha woke Thursday morning and went out to the barn to do her chores. Zoe neighed her greeting as she walked in the front door of the barn. Martha went over and patted her on the neck and then started to groom her.

After she fed the chickens, she hurried to the house to help Mom with breakfast. She started on slicing the bread and putting the butter on the table. "Where are the girls?"

"I don't know. They should have already been down here helping with breakfast. Would you please go check and see where they are?"

"Sure, Mom."

Martha hurriedly climbed the stairs and opened her bedroom door and what a sight there was. Sarah's hair was a mess; Lydia was trying to button her dress and Anna was trying unsuccessfully to dress Elizabeth. The two-year-old's curly hair was all a mess, her dress was on backwards, and she only had one arm through an arm hole.

"Girls, what are you doing? Mom had me come up and check on you because you're late getting to your chores."

"Sorry, Martha," exclaimed Anna. "I was trying to surprise you and spent so much time getting Elizabeth dressed that I kind of forgot to help Sarah and Lydia button their dresses."

"Well, I appreciate the thought, but it looks as if you got a little too much on your hands."

"I'm sorry, Martha," said Anna, starting to cry.

Martha hurriedly walked over to her sister and put a hand on her shoulder. "It's okay, Anna. You had good intentions and I really appreciate the thought. Come on, I'll help you fix things up and we can go down to breakfast together."

"Thank you."

Martha fixed Sarah's hair and put it in a ponytail and while Anna helped Lydia with her dress, Martha cleaned Elizabeth up and before long they were decent to go down to breakfast. Mom smiled as her daughter came in carrying Elizabeth with the others in tow.

About four o'clock that evening, the McShire family arrived and after saying her polite hello and shaking Mr. McShire's hand, she and Polly went to the kitchen to help finish up supper and talk.

"So, how have you been doing?"

"We've been doing fine, how about your family?"

"We're doing pretty well."

"Did you have a good Christmas?"

"Yes, we did. We had the Bear family over and they spent the night."

"Oh brother, I'm sure Francesca was a pain."

"Well, it wasn't the most pleasant time ever, but I tried to take this time to witness to her."

"You're right. I shouldn't have such an unkind attitude toward her. I really need to be praying for her."

"Yes, I think she's still hurting a lot from the move she's made. She left her best friend and what precious little of the faith she had in the Lord just vanished."

"That's so sad."

"Yes, I pray for her every time I think about her."

"That's a good idea. But, changing the subject, Tonya did the cutest thing on Christmas day."

"What was it?"

"Well, Tonya got a rag doll for Christmas and she was happily playing with it in the corner and while the rest of us were playing and looking at our toys we got for Christmas, she seemed to just disappear from the room. When I noticed she was gone, I went to check the other rooms. She is just starting to walk and had been all over the living room. I finally went upstairs to our room as a last resort. I was starting to get worried, but as I entered the hall, I could hear babbling as she was trying to sing to the melody of a lullaby that I sing to her every night. I followed the noise to our room and saw that she had climbed on the bed and she had tucked her rag doll under the blanket and was rocking back and forth babbling the lullaby. When she noticed me standing there, she stopped talking and pointed to her rag doll and then to herself."

"Oh, that is so adorable!"

"Yes, I sure thought it was."

"Let's get this food on the table." suggested Martha and the two girls started to set the table.

Everyone enjoyed a wonderful chicken with apple pie that was left over from Christmas, for dessert. Everyone also enjoyed each other's company.

As devotions were drawing to a close, Dad announced to the McShire family that in their family tradition, each child announces what verse they are going to focus on for the year. Their friends looked enthused and were very excited to see what verses the family chose.

Dad and Mom chose Sarah and Lydia's verses and Anna, who was now able to choose her verse, was so excited that she could hardly stay in her seat. When her turn finally came, she said she was going to be focusing on Proverbs 17:9 and after she recited it, it was James' turn.

Thomas was going before Martha and his verse was Romans 8:37 which states, *"Nay, in all these things we are more than conquerors through him who loved us."*

Martha thought that was a wonderful verse and Dad had to shake her gently to get her to the present.

"Martha, what's your verse?"

"Oh, sorry, my verse is Matthew 10:29-31 which states: *"Are not two sparrows sold for a farthing? and one of them shall not fall on the ground without your Father. But the very hairs of your head are all numbered. Fear ye not therefore, ye are of more value than many sparrows."*

"That's a wonderful verse, Martha. It reminds us not to be afraid and to put all our cares upon Him who loved, and still loves us," replied Mr. McShire.

"Thank you, Mr. McShire. I like the verse too."

"Martha, would you please choose a hymn?"

"Yes, sir," replied Martha to her father, "How about, "O God Our Help in Ages Past?"

"That's sounds like a good one."

At eleven fifty-five, the Knight and McShire families were standing and talking excitedly about the shortly coming year. Before long, it was eleven fifty-nine and soon, everyone was counting down.

"Ten...nine...eight...seven...six...five...four...three...two...ONE! Happy New Year!"

The husbands gave their wives a kiss and all the children gathered around holding hands as the adults joined their circle. Dad said a quick prayer, "Father, please help us to honor and glorify You this year, whatever You have in store for us. Please help us to rejoice always in Your love. In Your name we pray, amen."

Mom started singing:

"Praise to the Lord, the Almighty the King of creation!
O my soul, praise Him, for He is thy health and salvation!
All ye who hear, Now to His temple draw near; Join me in glad adoration!"

Then she started:

"O worship the King, all glorious above,
And gratefully sing His wonderful Love;
Our Shield and Defender the Ancient of days.
Pavilioned in splendor, and girded with praise."

Shortly after they were done singing, the McShire family left and Martha and Mom put the others to bed. They had to carry Elizabeth and Sarah, who had both fallen asleep, into their nice, warm beds.

After Martha was ready for bed, she got out her diary and recorded this joyous night and Christmas.

December 31, 1930 -- January 1, 1931

Dear God,

I had such a wonderful Christmas and New Year. We had the Bear family over for Christmas and it was quite fun. I tried to witness to

Francesca, but I'm not sure she was really listening. Please help me not to get discouraged, but help me to always give an answer for the hope that is in me. Please heal Francesca's hurting heart and draw her back to You in Your Own special time.

For New Year's, we had the McShire family over for dinner and devotions. It was so much fun.

Lord, help me to always trust You no matter what the circumstances. Keep my faith strong so that I can withstand the roughest storms. I love You SOOOO much.

Your Daughter,

Martha Rosemary Knight

Matthew 10:29-31
"Are not two sparrows sold for a farthing? and one of them shall not fall on the ground without your Father. But the very hairs of your head are all numbered. Fear ye not therefore, ye are of more value than many sparrows."

January 15th was Samuel Poltor and Grace Under's wedding day. The wedding was set for three o'clock and Martha was scurrying about, for it was already one p.m. and they were to leave at two-thirty. She was doing her sisters' hair and helping to dress them. She had Sarah done and she was sitting in a chair fidgeting with the strings on her dress; when Martha scolded her gently, Sarah replied, "But I don't like to sit forever and ever. I'm bored."

"Well, here's a picture book you can look at," she replied, handing her a book and then going back to tying a ribbon in Lydia's hair.

After she had Lydia dressed, she set her to look at another book and settled down to do Anna's hair.

Anna's blonde hair, barely past the shoulder, curled slightly, and you could do anything with it. So Martha decided to pull a little bit back and curl a few pieces of hair to make it look nice.

Finally, it was time for Martha to do up herself. She pulled her hair back into a low pony-tail and curled her hair, then put her nicer dress on.

After one last look at her sisters, making sure their bows were all tied and everything, they went downstairs and Martha told her sisters to stay put in the living room while she helped her Mom finish up Elizabeth so her mother could dress.

"Thank you, Martha," Mom replied gratefully when she offered to take over. "You look lovely," and she kissed her on the cheek.

They arrived at the church where the

ceremony was to take place. Martha helped her sisters out of the wagon and they were led to their seats. Just as Martha finished retying Sarah's strings, Mary and Cara Poltor appeared and gave her a hug. "You two look beautiful!"

"Thank you. We are bridesmaids."

"That is awesome; I'm so glad! Is Samuel nervous?"

"Oh yes, he hardly ate anything last night at supper," replied Mary, giggling.

"Well, I know they are going to make a marvelous couple."

They chatted for a few minutes more and then Martha exclaimed, "I think I see your mother waving to get your attention. You'd better see what she wants."

"Oh yes, see you after the ceremony."

Cathryn and Rose Williams were sitting in front of Martha, so they chatted till Mr. Poltor interrupted everyone and exclaimed, "The ceremony is about to begin, but first, I'd like to pray for the couple that is about to be married. If we will all bow our heads."

Everyone did so.

"Dear Heavenly Father, we thank You that You have brought this young couple together in marriage. May their life be long and fruitful together and let their love for each other grow into something magnificent and let them shine for You, Lord. Please bless our time together and let our speech be a blessing to each other. In Your Son's most holy Name, amen."

Pastor Share stood at the altar and Samuel appeared, standing beside him.

Annalise, Grace Under's sister, who was seven, was the flower girl and she walked forward, slowly pulling flower petals from her basket and dropping them on the floor.

Then came Mary and behind her, Cara, walking slowly down the aisle. Martha could see tears in Mary's eyes. She supposed that they were because her brother was getting married and they wouldn't see each other as often. Cara, on the other hand, was all smiles as she walked down the aisle and she gave a wink to Martha as she passed her.

Then came the matron of honor, Grace's older, married sister named Joyce and then following was the bride herself. She looked so pretty as she walked down on her father's arm. Her eyes were fixed on the groom and she was smiling.

The ceremony was beautiful. After the vows were exchanged and Pastor Share declared them man and wife, the couple kissed and turned to greet their friends as the new Mr. and Mrs. Samuel Poltor.

As everyone visited with each other after the ceremony, Samuel and Grace went around greeting everybody and thanking them for coming. Martha went and found Mary and Cara, who were chatting with Polly and Selah McShire.

Martha could tell there were tear tracks where Mary had been crying softly during the marriage and Martha slipped her arm about her friend's shoulders and whispered in her ear, "It's going to be okay."

Mary nodded, smiled and laid her head gently on her shoulder and sighed.

Martha looked around for Elizabeth, but she didn't see her. She shrugged her shoulders and assumed she was with Mom or one of her sisters.

The girls got some cookies and sat down at a table to eat them. They watched the bride and groom walking around and Martha saw how happy they looked. Samuel glancing at his wife every now and then with a loving and proud look that Martha thought to herself: *That's what I want my husband to be like.*

After finishing her snack, Martha went in search to find Grace and when she found her talking with Janelle Share, she waited patiently. When she was finished, she said, "Oh Mrs. Poltor, I'm so happy for you!"

"Thanks, Martha, but you can keep calling me Grace, at least till I get used to the name 'Poltor,'" and she laughed a happy laugh that made Martha's heart warm with happiness for her friend.

"So, are you and Samuel almost finished with your house?"

"Yes, the house is almost finished. It should be move-in ready at the beginning of February. Meanwhile, we'll stay with Jim and Laura."

"That's a good plan. Well, I see my Mom waving me over. I think we're getting ready to leave, but these last few hours were ones I'll never forget. Congratulations!"

"Thank you, Martha!" she replied, giving her a hug.

Martha walked over to her Mom and said, "What is it, Mom?" as she saw the worried look on her face.

"Oh, nothing maybe. Have you seen Elizabeth?"

"No. I haven't seen her since after the ceremony. Why? I thought she was with you."

"No. I thought she was with you," she exclaimed, as a look of worry clouded her face. "Does Dad have her?"

"No, I don't think so. Will you find Anna and ask her if she's seen her?"

"Sure, Mom."

Martha hurried to find Anna, who was in a corner chatting with Selah.

"Anna, have you seen Elizabeth?"

"No, I haven't. I thought you had her."

By now Martha was really getting worried. Her legs began to feel weak as she looked around the dimly lit room. She thoroughly searched the room with her eyes, but to no avail. As she went to tell her Mom the worrying news, she muttered to herself, "Where is she?" as a feeling of horrible dread washed over her.

Chapter 7
Where's Elizabeth?

Martha told her Mom the bad news, then she asked Polly and Rose to help her search for her sister. They agreed and spread out searching high and low for the lost little girl.

Martha was really worried, *What if she went outside? No, she couldn't have. She couldn't have opened the door; she isn't tall enough. Could she have opened a window and climbed out?* Martha was thoroughly scared and she grasped a chair to keep from falling to the floor. She decided to pray. "Dear Jesus, please help us to find Elizabeth. I'm really scared. Please protect her and please help her to stay where she is. Please help me to stay calm. In Jesus' Name, amen."

Martha checked under all the tables, but no Elizabeth. She checked in every dark corner, but no Elizabeth. She checked all the windows, but every one of them was locked and still no Elizabeth. She sighed with worry as she looked around. "Martha," said Polly coming up to her, "Tonya's missing, too. I wonder if Elizabeth is with her?"

"Uh-oh, I wonder what kind of trouble they can get into together? Come on, let's check the church pantry."

"Okay. Good idea," replied Polly.

They went to the pantry and opened the door and looked in every corner, but still no girls. "Where could they have disappeared to? They couldn't have gone out the door; they aren't tall enough to turn the door knob. I checked all the windows; they're all locked."

"Did you check this one?" asked Polly pointing to the little window in the pantry.

The little window was a small one and not big enough for girls like Polly and Martha to fit through. But it was big enough for girls like Elizabeth and Tonya. Martha shivered, "Boy, it's cold in here," as she walked to the window.

"No wonder, it's cracked!" exclaimed Polly.

Martha gasped, "No, it can't be! It just can't."

"I think so!"

"Are you thinking what I am?" asked Martha.

"I think I am," she said weakly.

"Let's go tell our parents. We'll meet back here in five minutes."

"All right," replied Polly.

Martha went to find her parents and told them what she thought had happened and Mom sobbed as she heard. "Oh Peter, she's lost! She can't be out there very long without her coat! She's going to die!"

"No; we'll find her sweetheart. Martha, show us to the pantry. I hope there are footprints."

They hurried to the pantry and sure enough, there were two sets of little footprints and hand prints as they half-crawled and walked to wherever they were going.

"Okay honey, you go find Michael and Janelle Share, stay with her and tell Michael to meet me outside of the church. Martha, put your coat on; we could use your help too."

"Okay, Dad," Martha was glad that she was able to help.

She put on her coat and scarf, stepped outside and shivered against the cold and wondered how long her two-year-old sister could bear this thirty-degree weather without any coat or scarf. She hurried around the building to the pantry window and looked where the footprints led.

She decided to go ahead and follow the prints and she was beyond sight of the church when her father and a few other men came out of the building. Dad looked but didn't see Martha. It only made him worry more, but he decided he would have to talk about it with her later and hoped that she was okay.

Martha followed the prints into the woods and looked up at the sky. It looked as if it would snow soon, but she ignored the serious warning and went ahead.

The footprints stopped at a log and Martha sat on it and thought where her sister and young friend could be. Then she noticed the log was moving a little bit. Her heart leaped for joy, hoping that it was her sister, but was sadly disappointed when she saw it was only a squirrel vibrating the log. She looked for more foot prints, but didn't see any.

It had started to snow and Martha was getting more and more worried about her sister. She prayed that God would be her and her sister's strength and shield and felt that she should head south and travel a little ways.

It wasn't long till she came to a big oak tree and when she approached it; she started to hear some soft crying. Martha ran and looked behind the tree and there were Elizabeth and Tonya, clutching at each other to try to stay warm. When Elizabeth spotted Martha she stood up and walked as quickly as her chubby legs could carry her and she held onto her skirt as if she wouldn't let go.

Martha lifted her in her arms and hugged her. Then noticing that it was snowing considerably harder now, she put Tonya on her back and Elizabeth on her hip and started toward the church again.

After walking for a while, she was starting to get worried and wished that she had paid more attention to where she was going, but that couldn't be helped now and she prayed that she could make it back safely.

Tonya had started to cry because she was cold, but Elizabeth lay her head on her sister's chest, seeming to know that it was all out of her hands and seemed to know that she had done wrong.

Martha was praying all the while that God would get them back safely. She kept murmuring to herself that the Lord was her strength and shield.

She had been walking for fifteen minutes, and as she rounded a corner, she saw her dad and some of the men. She sighed in relief and hurried back with them to the church, thanking God that He had protected her.

As she stepped through the front door, Mom saw them immediately and took action. She took Elizabeth from Martha's arms and Mrs. McShire took Tonya and they both hurried them to the wood stove to warm them up.

Polly took Martha's coat and scarf and hung them up and then seated her at a table and gave her a cup of hot cocoa.

A few hours later, the Knight family arrived home and the children were put to bed. Martha was about to retire to her own room when her father's voice beckoned her to come to him. "Yes Dad?"

"You did something very foolish today. Do you know what that was?"

Martha hung her head and nodded. "Yes, Dad, I do. I should've waited till you and the others were ready to search for Elizabeth and Tonya instead of going by myself. I was wrong and I regret that I did it. I hope I will never do the like again. Will you forgive me?"

"Yes, Martha, of course I forgive you, but your mother and I have to punish you to make sure you will make wise decisions in the future."

"Yes, Dad."

"From now on, till we tell you otherwise, you will have to tell either your mother or I where you are going—even if it's just to the barn."

"Yes, sir."

"We love you, and we want you to grow into a

woman that can make wise decisions, not hasty ones. You may go to bed now."

"Yes, sir; goodnight," and kissing her parents goodnight she headed to bed thinking that this was not a good way to start off the New Year.

Chapter 8
Oncoming Storm

January 19th came and so did Sarah's birthday. Martha got up early to make a special treat for her sister's birthday.

She dressed and came downstairs and started making chocolate muffins for breakfast. They were Sarah's favorite and a rare treat in the Knight home.

She had gotten permission from her Mom to make them. So she got the necessary ingredients and mixed them together in a batter.

Next, she poured the batter into a muffin tin and popped it into the oven to bake. Then, leaving Mom close by to watch the muffins, she put on her coat and scarf and hurried to the barn to do her chores. Her Dad and brothers were already there.

"Good morning, Dad."

"Good morning, daughter. Did you get the muffins in the oven?"

"Yes, but how did you know?"

"Your mother told me," he replied with a smile.

Martha got to work feeding the chickens and

horses and then gathered some wood for the wood box. She also decided to bless Sarah by taking her chore of setting the table.

About an hour or so later, everyone had sat down to eat. After they were finished, Anna and Lydia started to clear the table.

Martha and Sarah went to gather all the hymnals for devotions. "Thank you for setting the table for me. It was really nice being able to sleep in later."

"You're welcome. I'm glad I could do it for you!" she said giving her a hug. "By the way, are you excited about turning four?"

"Oh yes, I've really been looking forward to it!"

"Come on, let's go and set these hymnals in the living room."

After lunch, Martha laid Sarah and Elizabeth down for a nap. Then she went and took a book that she was reading and sat by the fire in the living room to read for a bit.

About a half hour later, she closed the book and laid it aside and tiptoed up to her room and went softly in. She reached under her bed and felt around for something.

Recently, Martha had made her sister a book with all the numbers up to one hundred and she wanted to wrap it. But as she was about to lift it up from under the bed, she saw a pair of eyes watching her. They belonged to Sarah!

Martha was startled and slipped the gift under her skirt and smiled at her sister. "You're not supposed to be awake."

"Sorry, I just had trouble sleeping. What are you doing under the bed?"

"Oh, just checking something and now that I've checked it, I'm going out now." She slipped out before her sister could say anything and sighed as she closed the door and whispered to herself,

"Whew; that was close!"

She went and got some wrapping paper from a drawer in the kitchen. She also got some scissors and tape. Then she went to the living room and wrapped the little book up and set it on the mantle where all the other gifts were.

Mom was working on the birthday cake and Martha went and asked if she could do anything. "You could make the frosting," was the reply and Martha got the ingredients to make chocolate frosting, which was her sister's favorite.

About an hour later, everyone was crowded in the living room around Sarah; she was opening her presents and Elizabeth had claimed her spot beside Sarah and was clapping her hands in delight.

Sarah got some new coloring supplies and she squealed in delight as she saw all of the colors.

"Oh, thank you, Mommy; I can't wait!"
When Sarah got to Martha's gift, she cried in delight, "Now I won't forget!"

Martha was glad that Sarah was having a wonderful birthday and hoped she would be with them for many more years.

The next day there were clouds and by lunch time, it was snowing furiously. Lydia and Sarah were both looking out the window and they both had a look that was tired of all the snow. They couldn't wait for spring. Anna, on the other hand, exclaimed: "I love winter and all the snow; it means not as many chores and I get to sit here by the fire and work on my school."

"Well, I can't wait for spring," replied Martha. "Spring is the start of everything new. The flowers are in bloom and the trees are growing new leaves. And the air is so fresh."

"Well, I guess if you look at it that way, spring can be very welcoming, but just the same, winter is my favorite season," Anna retorted playfully.

Martha closed her math book with a sigh. She did really well with English, but math was the one subject that she didn't like very well. She moved on to her history and by four o'clock, she had all her school done and was able to help her mother with supper.

Martha started slicing the bread while Mom was stirring some hot soup and going on about how long this winter would last and how cold it was. "I sure hope spring arrives earlier than usual, but with all the snow we've gotten, I'm doubtful," exclaimed Mom.

"Yes, one thing I'm looking forward to is writing Irene Williams again. Since we don't go to town in the winter very much, I can't mail her any letters."

"I'm sorry. But hopefully you'll be able to write to her soon. I'm sure it will be a very long letter," Mom sympathized.

"Yes, I think it will be. I better call the girls in to help set the table," replied Martha.

After supper and devotions, the boys bundled up to go out and do the barn chores. Martha asked to go with them and when she had gotten permission, she hurried, put on her coat and followed them out to the barn. Martha fed the horses and the boys raked out the stalls while Dad milked and fed Cassie the cow.

About twenty minutes later, Martha and the boys were ready to go back to the house. Dad told them to stay close together and hold on to the rope. Martha was behind Thomas and she was fine for a bit, but then her feet and hands got numb and she was blocking her face against the wind and snow.

Before she knew it, she couldn't see the boys any longer and she realized her hands were not on the rope anymore. She became scared and looked around. She couldn't see anything. Not even a light from the house.

She groped in the dark, trying her hardest to find the rope and when she couldn't, she dropped to the ground in a pile of snow in desperation.

A minute later, she remembered that her father had said never to sit and rest in snow, keep moving to keep your circulation going. She prayed that God would help her find her home and chose a direction and stayed at it.

She finally came to a tree and found that she was probably in the woods. She decided that there was no hope that she would find her way back now, but decided to keep going. The McShire's couldn't live very far away and Martha just hoped she was heading in the right direction.

She got tired after a while and came to a log and sat down upon it. She felt her eyes grow tired and start to droop and she just wanted to sleep, but she decided she needed to push on and hurried in the same direction.

About an hour later, she stumbled upon a light. She hoped it was the McShire's and she went up on the porch and knocked. She had to knock several times to be heard and when she finally was, she saw it was not the McShire home as she had hoped, but it was the Bear home.

Mrs. Bear looked astonished as she pulled Martha in and started to take her coat off. "Daniel! Come here!"

When he entered the room, he too, looked surprised. But he acted quickly and set a chair beside the fire and set her on it. Martha shivered furiously and rubbed her hands to get them to come alive again.

Mrs. Bear got her a cup of hot chocolate and Martha wrapped her fingers around the warm cup and tried to smile gratefully, but her lips could hardly move. She thanked God that He had taken care of her and that He had brought her to a warm place against this blizzard.

Mr. and Mrs. Bear had insisted that she sleep there that night, despite how worried her parents would be and by the next morning, the snow had stopped and Martha wanted to be getting home to her family.

So Mr. Bear hitched up their team of horses and helped her into the sleigh and before Martha knew it, they pulled into her own yard again and Martha jumped down and into her parents' arms. Mom was crying with relief and all her siblings gathered around her talking at the same time and hugging her.

Mr. Bear stayed for about an hour and then, after seeing him off, went inside to hear the story once again.

Chapter 9
Strength and Shield

Martha felt very grateful that the Lord had helped her find shelter that night when she got lost. But she put all that behind her and stepped forward.

Elizabeth, who was now tottering on her chubby baby legs, tugged on Martha's skirt and pointed toward the cookie bowl, saying, "Have one?"

"Yes, you may have one. Here you go; sit down at the table to eat it, though."

"'Twank you,'" Elizabeth replied happily.

Martha shook her head. She couldn't believe how fast her sister was growing up. Martha put the cookie dough she had been making onto a sheet pan and put them in the oven. She grabbed a cookie and seated herself beside Elizabeth who was just taking the last bite of hers. She hopped off the chair and slowly tottered away to the living room.

Martha finished her cookie and set to work on writing an essay for history. Not long after she started, the new batch of cookies was done and Martha pulled them out of the oven just as Thomas and James stepped in from the back door. Martha just stared at them and exclaimed, "How come you always come in exactly when I pull cookies out?"

Thomas just laughed and grabbed one, "Ouch! They're hot!"

"Well, they just came out of the oven, silly!"

"No wonder," he replied and sucked on his fingers.

"Why don't you sit down and warm up? I'll get some hot chocolate and by that time the cookies will have cooled down some."

The boys sat down and took off their coats and scarves. "Why are you in so early? I thought you were helping Dad in the barn?" asked Martha.

"We were, but Dad said we could take a twenty minute break. It's pretty cold out there, you know."

"How's Zoe doing?" asked Martha.

"She's fine, as always." replied James teasingly.

"I meant about her foal."

"Oh, she's fine. I guess. Awfully round, though."

"Stop teasing."

"Okay then, she's fine. Dad thinks she'll drop

her foal by middle of April."

"That's good."

Martha poured hot chocolate into two cups and handed them to the boys and then put the cookies on a plate and set it on the table, saying, "Enjoy boys, I'm going to the living room to sew a tear that I accidentally made in one of my dresses the other day."

"Okay, have fun," replied James poking fun at his sister.

Martha pulled a chair up close to the fire and got a needle and thread and set to fixing the tear that she had made. She had just set the needle in her lap and had thought what tedious work sewing was when she heard a thump, kerplunk, thump...thump that sounded as if it came from the stairs. By the time Martha got there, Anna had burst into tears and was holding her ankle as tears were streaming down her face.

"Mom, Anna's hurt. I think she fell down the stairs!"

Mom came running from her room and lifted Anna into her lap and asked what happened. "I-I w-was carrying d-down my s-sewing basket and I tripped over one of Elizabeth's t-toys."

"I'm sorry about that. Let's get you to the

living room so we can take a look at that ankle; Lydia, would you please go and ring the bell on the back porch? That will signal your father for me."

"Yes, ma'am."

Dad came immediately to see his daughter's ankle and pronounced that he didn't think it was broken, but it was definitely badly sprained. He announced that she should stay off her leg for a few days to give it a chance to heal. He said he would make her some crutches so she could move around.

"You're very blessed, young lady, that it wasn't broken. Who left the toy on the stairs?"

"Elizabeth," Anna replied grimacing with pain.

"Elizabeth, dear," called Mom to her young daughter. "You shouldn't leave your toys out like that."

"Sowwy Mum" she replied. She walked clumsily over to her sister. "I'm sowwy Anna, I twy not to lef my toys out agin."

"It's okay, Elizabeth. I know you didn't mean to. Would you like to play a puzzle with me?"

"Yes!" replied Elizabeth with a smile.

Martha put her sewing stuff away and went to

get a pillow for Anna's sore foot. She propped up her sister's leg on it and the nine-year-old smiled gratefully and set to finishing the puzzle she and Elizabeth were doing.

Martha looked at the clock and saw that it was already four o'clock and it was time to start supper.

She went to the kitchen and set a pot on the stove and set to making a warm stew. When she had finished that, it was four thirty. She called Lydia and Sarah to help set the table while she cut the bread.

By the time supper was ready, Lydia and Sarah were running around the kitchen playing tag. Martha told them to stop and sit down at the table, but they supposedly didn't hear and kept playing.

She asked a second time, but nothing happened. She was running out of patience and finally stamped her foot on the ground and yelled, "Stop it you two and sit down at the table!"

"Sorry, Martha," replied Lydia, with one more little laugh.

"Go sit at the table."

Lydia and Sarah started toward the table, but Sarah gave Lydia one more little push and Lydia accidentally lost her balance. She reached out her hand and touched the wrong thing—the hot stove! She let out a cry of pain and took it away quickly. "Ow-ow-ow!" Tears were streaming down her face as she held her hand.

"Sarah, go and get some rags and soak them in water while I get the butter."

Sarah immediately obeyed, knowing that she had done something wrong. Martha examined her sister's hand. It was very red and blisters were starting to form on the burn. By now Mom had arrived. She had been changing Elizabeth's diaper when it happened.

She looked at the hand and immediately called for Dad, who was in the living room reading, to come and look. Sarah handed her mother the wet rags and Martha placed the butter on the table. Martha knew this was going to hurt badly, so she pulled her sister into her lap and squeezed her tightly to keep her still.

Lydia screamed when the rag touched her burns and her tears fell rapidly on Martha's arms while she still held her tight. "I'm so sorry, baby. But I have to clean it out." Mom soothingly explained. "Sarah, hand me the butter."

After Dad had looked at it, Mom wrapped it up and Martha still held her and asked, "Are you hungry?" Lydia shook her head 'no' and said weakly, "I'm tired."

"Martha, would you take her up to bed, please?"

"Yes."

Martha carried her sister upstairs and helped her into her night gown, brushed her hair and tucked her into bed, putting another quilt over her and kissing her forehead.

After Martha ate her supper, she got her Bible and sat by the fire reading and thinking.

Slowly, she closed the Bible and thought: *God sure has taken good care of us. He protected Elizabeth, Tonya, and me. He protected me when I got lost. He protected Thomas and me from getting the flu. And He protected Anna and Lydia from getting hurt too badly. Now that's protection. He's been our Strength and Shield this whole time. It's amazing to think of the good care and protection He's given to us.*

She prayed a short prayer, thinking how good He was and she was smiling to herself when there was a scream. It came from upstairs and Martha said with a groan, "Not again." She hurriedly put her Bible on the mantle and ran up the stairs with Mom right behind her.

Martha threw open the door and they saw that Lydia was sitting up in bed screaming.

Martha and Mom comforted Lydia and
started waking her up from her dream. "Lydia,"
soothed Mom, "it's okay. Mommy's here. You're
just having a bad dream."

Mom continued to gently wake her from the
bad dream, but Lydia continued screaming. "Please
get me a cup of water, James," commanded Mom.

A minute later, James arrived with a cup of
water and Mom held it in her hand for when her
daughter awakened. Soon, Lydia came back to
reality, but she seemed to know nothing of what
happened. "Mommy," she said weakly, "my head
hurts."

"You had a bad dream. Here's a drink of
water. Martha will sleep with you tonight. I think
she's about ready for bed anyway," she replied,
looking at Martha pointedly.

Martha understood and nodded her head.

"Okay Mommy, but I don't remember any
bad dream."

About ten minutes later, Lydia and Martha
were in bed and Martha sighed and whispered to
herself, "Strength and Shield," and closed her eyes
and slept.

Chapter 10
Long Winter

The next afternoon, Mom and Dad checked on Lydia's burned hand. Martha stood quietly beside the bed, talking quietly to her sister to hopefully help distract her. Martha noticed her mother look up at her father. As Lydia ate a few crackers with cheese, Martha followed her parents out of the door.

"Do you think we should take her to the doctor, Peter?" asked Mom.

Dad nodded, "I think so. I'm sure that Lydia will be fine; I just want the doctor to look at her hand. We'll travel into Helena and get her checked at the hospital there."

"All right, honey," assented Mom, "I'll gather things together and we'll head out."

As Mom disappeared, Dad turned to his eldest daughter, "I'm not sure how long we'll be, dear. You're in charge of things until we get back, okay?"

Martha, with a worried look on her face, nodded. "Will Lydia be okay?"

"I truly think so, but as I told your mother, I'd feel better if I had the doctor look at her hand. I think she may need some medicine to help the burn heal. We'll see."

"Yes sir."

Martha hurried downstairs and gathered her siblings together in the living room to see their parents and sister off. Sarah started to cry because she knew that she was responsible for Lydia's burn. Martha reminded herself to talk with her after they left.

Mom kissed her children goodbye and Dad gave instructions to the boys. "Don't worry, Dad," said Thomas, "I'll take care of everyone." He puffed out his chest.

"I know you can, son, just remember to obey Martha."

"Yes sir." Thomas saluted his father before stepping back.

As Dad and Mom left in the wagon with Lydia, Martha turned to her siblings. "Why don't we try to surprise Lydia when she comes back?"

"What do you think we should do?" pondered Anna.

"Why don't we draw her pictures?" asked James.

"Good idea, James," agreed Anna. "Maybe we

could also make her favorite sweet treat!"

"I think those are some great ideas, everyone!" exclaimed Martha. "Thomas, would you gather the paper and colors and such?"

"Sure, sis!" Thomas hurried in the direction of the supplies with Anna and James in tow. As they disappeared from the room, Martha sat down on the couch and pulled Sarah up onto her lap. "What's wrong, honey?"

"I-It's my f-fault that Lydia has to go to the h-hospital." Sarah hiccupped as she told her sister.

Martha sighed as she hugged her sister. "I know it was an accident, Sarah, but because you disobeyed me, Lydia does have the burn and has to go to the doctor."

"I'm sorry, Martha. I wish I had obeyed what you told me."

Martha smiled at Sarah, "I'm glad you're sorry, Sarah. Have you asked God to forgive you?"

Sarah shook her head.

"Well, then, why don't you do that right now and then we'll go and begin coloring?"

Sarah nodded as she folded her hands and bowed her head. "Dear God, I'm sorry for not obeying Martha yesterday and I'm sorry I accidentally hurt Lydia. Would you please forgive me and help me to do better? Please make my big sister feel better. In Jesus' Name I pray, amen."

"Amen! Good job, sis," encouraged Martha. "Now, why don't you go and join the others in the kitchen? I'll be along shortly."

Sarah skedaddled off and Martha straightened up the living room as a knock sounded on the front door. Martha quickly peaked out the front window and noticed that it was Leslie McShire.

Martha opened up the door and smiled, "How are you, Mrs. McShire?"

"I'm doing well, though I'm sorry to hear about your sister."

Martha smiled kindly, "Thank you, but how did you know?"

"Oh, your parents dropped by the house and told us what happened. I came over here to stay with you all until your parents get back."

"That's very nice of you, Mrs. McShire; thank you so much!"

"No problem! It's what neighbors do for each other."

Mrs. McShire hung her coat and scarf up. "Where are your siblings? It's awful quiet in this house."

"They're drawing pictures for Lydia when she returns and later, we're going to make her favorite sweet treat."

"That sounds fun!" Leslie McShire walked into the kitchen where Martha began washing the lunch dishes. "I'll dry the dishes, dear."

"Thank you."

"No problem. By the time we're finished here, the others will be done coloring and we can start baking away!"

Martha looked kindly up at her friend and prayed to Jesus, *Thank You, oh Lord, for providing for us yet again. Please heal Lydia's hand and help it not to be very painful. In Your Name I pray, amen.*

Chapter 11
Waiting

It was late when Dad and Mom got home with Lydia. James held the door open for his parents and Dad entered carrying a very tired looking Lydia. Sarah quickly followed him up the stairs and Martha took her mother's coat and scarf. "What did the doctor say, Mom?"

"Well," Mom began, sitting down on the couch. "It was a pretty bad burn, but the doctor gave us a special salve to put on the burn area and we're supposed to keep it cleanly wrapped and to keep an eye on it for infection. The doctor says she'll be fine."

"Oh good!" exclaimed Martha.

Leslie McShire said her goodbyes and after a thorough round of thank-you's she hurried home. As Mom got up to begin putting her stuff away, she seriously told her children, "We're going to have to be very patient with Lydia. The next few days are going to be very difficult and painful for her as her burn heals. So, just remember to be patient and kind."

"Yes, Mom, we will." Thomas answered for all of them.

Martha headed up the stairs to see how her sister was getting settled in. When she entered the room with Anna, Lydia was being covered up in bed and Sarah was sitting right beside her devotedly, holding the hand that wasn't bandaged up.

"How are feeling, Lydia?" asked Anna softly.

"I-I don't feel too good right now. My burn hurts. T-Thank you for asking me, though."

Martha sympathetically smoothed her sister's dark hair out of her face. "We all wanted to do something special for you, sis; so we all drew pictures for you and made your favorite sweet treat—brownies!"

"Sarah showed me the pictures, but I didn't know about the brownies. Daddy," Lydia turned her attention to her father, "may I have a brownie right now?"

Dad smiled at his young daughter, "Well...I know it's late, but you've had a long day so I think a brownie would be a special treat. Martha, would you please fetch a brownie for Lydia?"

"Sure, Dad, I'll be right back."

Martha hurried down the stairs, happy she could do something for her sister.

Lydia was soon enjoying her brownie and then she went into a peaceful sleep with Sarah snuggled up beside her; still holding her hand.

The next day, Lydia was feeling a little better, but the burn was still hurting. As Martha and Sarah came in with a tray consisting of a sandwich and a cookie, and Sarah very carefully carrying a cool glass of lemonade, Lydia looked up at them grumpily. "Did you make me a peanut butter and jelly sandwich?"

"Yes, dearie, we did." Martha replied cheerily.

"You didn't put too much jelly on it, did you?" whined Lydia.

Martha smiled as she set the small tray down upon Lydia's lap. "I made your sandwich just how you like it, more peanut butter than jelly on it."

"Good." Lydia picked up the sandwich and took a bite of it.

As Lydia was still chewing, she demanded, "Where's my drink?!"

"Sarah has it, Lydia."

Sarah approached just then and handed the glass of lemonade to her sister. "Here you go."

Lydia nodded and muttered a 'thank you' and sipped the sweet drink. Martha gave Sarah a wink that encouraged her to continue being patient.

As Lydia finished her meal, she snuggled down under her covers and decided she wanted to take a nap. Martha sat beside her and stroked her arm lovingly. "What are you thinking about, sweetie?" asked Martha.

"How long do you suppose it will take for my burn to heal?"

Martha pondered carefully, "Probably a few weeks, dearie."

"My burn hurts, Martha."

"I know. Hopefully, it won't hurt for much longer. The salve should help the healing process."

"So, it won't hurt the whole time it's healing?"

"No, I don't think so. It'll probably only hurt for a few more days."

"Okay. I'm glad about that."

There was a moment of silence and then a very sleepy Lydia asked, "Would you please sing to me? I like it when you sing. You have a nice voice."

"Sure, I will, dear. What would you like me to sing?"

"'Jesus Loves Me'; that's my favorite."

"Okay." Martha began to sing.

*"Jesus loves me this I know,
for the Bible tells me so,
little ones to Him belong,
they are weak but He is strong.
Yes, Jesus loves me! Yes, Jesus loves me!
Yes, Jesus loves me! The Bible tells me so.*

*Jesus loves me! This I know,
For the Bible tells me so.
Taking children on His knee, saying,
Let them come to Me.*

*Jesus loves me! He will stay
Close beside me on my way.
He's prepared a home for me,
And someday His face I'll see.*

*Yes, Jesus loves Me! Yes, Jesus loves me!
Yes, Jesus loves me! The Bible tells me so."*

As Martha finished the song, she thought that Lydia was asleep, but as she stood up, Lydia asked in a very sleepy voice, "Martha, would you pray that God would heal my burn quickly?"

"Yes, I certainly will dearie."

Both girls bowed their heads and Martha held Lydia's hand, "Dear Lord Jesus, please be with Lydia and her hurt hand. I pray that You heal it very quickly and help it not to hurt. Please help Lydia be patient as it heals. In Jesus' Name we pray, amen."

"Thank you, Martha."

"You're very welcome. I love you!"

"I love you, too!"

Lydia's burn healed quickly and within a few days, she was feeling more like her usual self. Her burn healed completely within a few weeks and Lydia was grateful when the bandage could come off. The Knight family praised God for Lydia's smooth healing.

On a brisk day in early February, Martha was coming in from the barn when she looked up to see a wagon rolling up the drive. She saw that it was the Bear family.

Martha prayed that she might, once again, be a witness to Francesca. But sometimes she was very difficult to deal with. Remembering that Miss Bear was in a hard predicament, she prayed that the Lord would give her the patience to cope with her new found friend.

Martha walked up to greet them as they arrived at the house and helped Jenny down and said to Francesca, "Do you want to come to the barn with me? Our mare is pregnant and she's very friendly. And my pet cat, Jubilee, is in the barn and you can pet her."

"Sure, I guess. My parents wanted to drop off some clothes that don't fit Jenny anymore that would probably fit one of your younger sisters."

"That's great. Come on, let's race to the barn."

"Okay!"

The girls arrived at the barn and Jubilee got up from her spot on a bale of hay and went to Martha and weaved in and out around her legs. Martha picked her up and handed her to Francesca.

She petted her gently around the ears and she purred loudly. "She likes you!" exclaimed Martha.

Francesca giggled, "I guess she does, doesn't she?"

Martha walked over to the mare and patted her gently on her round tummy. "Come here, you can sometimes feel the foal moving."

Francesca walked over and laid her hand next to Martha's. "I felt a kick!" she replied, quickly removing her hand.

The two girls sat on a hay bale and chatted for a while when Francesca said, "This barn looks pretty new. Have you recently built it?"

"That's quite a story. You see, in September I think it was, a tornado ruined most of our crops and tore down the barn. Our neighbors helped us build another barn so that's why it looks new."

"Oh," was the one word Francesca replied with, but suddenly, a minute later, she burst out. "How CAN you still trust God when everything around you is ruined and the world has turned upside down on you?"

"I wondered about that for a long time, and I still don't know why He lets these things happen, but I think a lot of it is to test our faith. You see, it's easy to trust God when everything is going smoothly. It's when your whole world is crumbling that you have to put your faith and trust to work in the Lord; having faith that He will take care of you." Martha patted Francesca's shoulder comfortingly before she continued. "It's hard and I struggled with that problem for a while. But then I realized that I couldn't do it on my own. I needed to confide in somebody and that somebody was Jesus, my Deliverer."

"Well, I just can't see why He had to move me away from my friends. I miss them terribly. I bet you never had to move away from your friends."

"No, I haven't. But you know, Francesca, in the Bible it says that there is a Friend that sticks closer than a brother. That Friend is Jesus. He's everything we need. You know the part in the Lord's Prayer where it says, "Give us this day our Daily Bread?"

"Yes, I don't know the prayer very well, but I recognize that part."

"That 'Daily Bread' is Jesus. He's enough. He's more than enough. We all have doubts, Francesca. I've had more doubts that 'Jesus will take care of me' than I can count or want to admit. I'm being a friend to you and that's why I'm telling you this. Turn all your cares upon Him, for He loves and cares for you. His heart is aching for you."

Just then, Mr. Bear poked his head in the barn and told Francesca that it was time to go.

Francesca got up without even a word to Martha and followed her Dad to the wagon.

Martha picked Jubilee up into her lap and sighed, "I hope I didn't offend her." She started singing softly, *"Jesus loves me. He will stay, close beside on my way, He's prepared a home for me! And some day His face I'll see."*

Chapter 12
What Then?

It was late at night and Martha had gone upstairs to bed. She put her nightgown on and crawled into bed and pulled the covers up to her chin. She tried going to sleep, but she wasn't tired. No matter how many times she adjusted her pillow, she still couldn't sleep.

Then she realized that she hadn't read her Bible that night like she usually did, so she lit a lamp and pulled her Bible out of the night table drawer and turned to James three and read for a while.

Finally, when she thought that she was tired enough, she put her Bible away and blew out the lamp and snuggled under the covers.

She was almost asleep when she heard voices downstairs. She didn't mean to eavesdrop, but she couldn't help but overhear what her parents were saying.

"Things are getting pretty bad here, Rosemary. I don't know how we're going to make it this next year."

"Well, I could reduce how much we eat each week and reduce our grocery bill. That would help some."

"Yes, I guess that would. But I'm not sure how much longer we can stretch the money."

"I know, dear. We just need to keep praying about it. When are you going to town again?"

"Probably as soon as next week."

"Well, I think we'll need more flour. Oh, would you get any mail we have at the post office?"

"Sure I will. I know Martha's anxious to start writing letters to her friend, Irene. I'll let her know that she'll need to be getting her first letter ready to send to her friend. Are you ready to go to bed, sweetheart?"

"Yes, I believe so."

And with that, Martha could hear her parents get ready for bed. She hadn't intended to hear what they were saying. She should've covered her ears, but she was so enraptured by what she had heard that she didn't think.

Oh, this was terrible. Would they have to move? Where would they go? These miserable questions were running through Martha's mind right then.

The next week dragged by for Martha. She was so worried about what might happen. She should've told her parents right away that she had heard and they would assure her that everything was working in God's plan, although they didn't know what that plan was yet.

Martha hurried to finish her letter to Irene and it ended like this:

Irene, pray for me. Money is short for us right now. I'm trying to trust Him, but it's really hard.

Write again soon!

Love, your friend and sister in Christ,

Martha

Martha hurried and tucked the letter into the envelope and went down the stairs and handed it to her father. She hugged him and told him to be careful. Thomas was going with him and after the sleigh had left, Martha went to start some more bread.

After supper, Thomas and Dad hadn't arrived home yet so everyone adjourned to the living room to listen for the bells on the sleigh.

"Mommy, why hasn't Daddy come home, yet?" asked Lydia.

"Well, with all the snow, it takes longer to get there and back, and with the snow melting, they have to be careful of the mud puddles. Poor Vernon and Zoe probably got stuck a few times," replied Mom.

"Good," said Lydia as she went back to her coloring.

Before long, to the relief of everyone in the room, came the sound of bells jingling. Mom got up and put her coat on and went to put Vernon and Zoe away in the barn. James got up to assist her while Martha went into the kitchen and put another piece of wood in the stove and to get the boys their supper.

Thomas came in, sighed and sat down at the supper table and started to eat his supper. Martha asked where the flour was so that she could put it away in the pantry. Thomas sighed again and replied, "We didn't get any flour."

"Why?"

"The prices were too high."

"Oh dear!"

"I know," replied Thomas. "Things aren't looking good, Martha. What happens if we run out of food? What then?"

Martha didn't know what to think. "G-God will take care of us. I know that. I'm just not sure how."

That night as Martha went to bed; she looked up her Bible verse for that year and read it to herself a few times over.

"Are not two sparrows sold for a farthing? and one of them shall not fall on the ground without your Father. But the very hairs of your head are all numbered. Fear ye not therefore, ye are of more value than many sparrows."

Lord, I don't know what you're doing with my life, but please help me to live for you! No matter what! And with that, she blew out the lamp and crawled under the covers.

Chapter 13
Moving On

March came around and by the middle of the month, Martha was feeling pretty good. It was no longer winter, but spring. Yes, the snow was still on the ground and it probably wouldn't be gone till April, but all was well. Or so Martha thought...

"Come on, Martha, let's go. We're going to be late for church!" urged Sarah, tugging on her sister's hand as Martha grabbed her Bible and bonnet and stepped out the door and into the sleigh. She figured this would be one of the last times she would ride in the sleigh till next winter.

Martha pulled Elizabeth into her lap and the sleigh set off with a lurch; Martha felt all happy and joyful inside. They arrived at the church shortly after and Dad let them off at the door and told them that he would be in as soon as he tied the horses up at the hitching rail.

Martha carried the lunch of soup inside and set it on a table in the far corner and went to chat with her friends with Elizabeth in tow, walking on her chubby legs. "Hi Francesca, how are you doing?"

"Fine; how about yourself?"

"We're good."

Francesca Bear had gotten friendlier towards Martha, but she was still unsure of herself and sometimes her temper would show, but she was getting better. Martha turned to Rose Williams and talked with her for a while until the service started.

Soon, Pastor Share called them to worship and they all started singing.

Oh God, our help in ages past
our Hope for years to come!
Our shelter from the stormy blast
and our Eternal Home!

Martha looked around at all her friends in turn. She caught the eye of Cathryn and as their eyes met, they smiled and Martha turned her face back to her hymn book.

After the service was concluded, Martha went to help the mothers get the meal ready. She got the forks, spoons, and napkins and set them at their places. She put a utensil in each dish, and then got Elizabeth's, Sarah's, and Lydia's lunch and went to find her friends.

She ended seeing Polly, and as Martha approached her, Polly exclaimed, "Francesca's attitude sure has changed dramatically. She's not as moody as she once was."

"Yes, she has changed a lot. I think a lot of it was her feelings about moving. She was blaming

God for moving her away from her friends. But I truly do think she has benefited from the move."

"I think so, too. Come on, let's go get our lunch; looks as though the girls are going through line now."

"Yes, let's go."

Later that night, Martha was working at drawing a picture with Anna. Sarah and Lydia were playing card games; the boys were studying for a test, and Mom and Dad were talking softly.

Martha asked to make a pot of hot chocolate, as the weather was still cold enough for some. After gaining permission, she warmed some milk and dumped some cocoa and sugar into it and stirred it around. Soon it was ready and she poured herself and Anna a cup and invited anybody who wanted some to come and get it before it was all gone.

After everyone had finished their hot chocolate, Dad and Mom called their children into the living room. Anna, Lydia, and Sarah sat at their feet and Martha in her mother's rocking chair holding Elizabeth.

"Your mother and I have something to announce to you all," Dad started slowly. "As you know, things have been pretty tight around here— especially money. We've been praying for the Lord to do His will in our lives and to do what He sees fit to give us."

Here he paused and Mom put her arm on his shoulder as if for comfort. He continued.

"The Lord has been very gracious to give us such a bountiful garden this past year that has provided us with enough food for the winter. But I'm not sure we can make it through the next year. The almanac has been saying we're going to have a very hard, dry summer this year for the crops. Therefore, I've been talking on the telephone to Mr. Williams, Irene's father, whenever I'm in town and he said there is some land near their place and that we could stay with them while we build."

He took a deep breath. "I don't want to leave this place. But I truly feel that God is moving us to Colorado, and so, in the first week of April, we will be moving to Colorado."

Martha let out a gasp. *Moving?* She thought. *This is terrible. I don't want to leave my friends. Lord, why are You letting this happen to us? Why?*

The younger girls had started crying softly and Thomas sat in his chair solemnly while James clapped his hands in excitement. "This is going to be quite an adventure! I can't wait!"

Mom had tears in her eyes and she was trying to hold them back. But in total misery, a tear slowly ran down her cheek. Dad hugged her close and she laid her head on his shoulder.

A while later, after everything had set in, Martha helped Mom put the younger girls to bed. Then Mom gave her daughter a hug and told her everything was going to be all right. God would take care of them.

Mom said goodnight and headed out of the room. Martha got ready for bed and then got her diary out and wrote in it.

March 15th, 1931,

Dear God,

My heart is aching. We children found out that we are moving to Colorado. Lord, I don't want to move. Why did You have to move us? Why? Help me to trust in You no matter what. Lord, I'm going to hold steady on to You because You're all that I have left.

Your Daughter,

Martha Rosemary Knight

The tears were falling fast on the page. Martha quickly closed her diary and crawled under the covers. She cried her heart out with tears running down her face. The thoughts that were running through her mind were: *Leave my friends—Polly, Cathryn, Rose, and so many others? How in the world can I live without them?*

Late that night, Martha wiped her eyes and nose, and finally went to bed with puffy red eyes and fell into a restless sleep.

Those would be the last tears that she would shed for a long while. Martha Rosemary Knight didn't know this yet, but she had entered into a great adventure that she would never forget.

The End!

Martha has just entered a very grand adventure. Will she accept the challenge or will she reject it?

Find out in book four of Martha Knight:

Martha's Rough Season

Made in the USA
Middletown, DE
19 April 2016